MINUS ONE

NIX
MINUS ONE

JILL MACLEAN

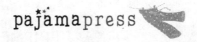

pajamapress

The publisher gratefully acknowledges the support of the Canada Council for the
Arts and the Ontario Arts Council for its publishing program. We acknowledge
the financial support of the Government of Canada through the Book Publishing
Industry Development Program (BPIDP) for our publishing activities.

 Canada Council   Conseil des Arts   ONTARIO ARTS COUNCIL
for the Arts   du Canada   CONSEIL DES ARTS DE L'ONTARIO

Library and Archives Canada Cataloguing in Publication

MacLean, Jill
    Nix minus one / Jill MacLean.

Issued also in electronic formats.
ISBN 978-1-927485-24-8 (bound).--ISBN 978-1-927485-25-5 (pbk.)

    I. Title.

PS8575.L415N59 2013   jC813'.6   C2012-907152-8

Cover and book design–Rebecca Buchanan
Woodchip (back cover)–Shutterstock/©R.S.Jegg

Pajama Press Inc.
469 Richmond St E, Toronto Ontario, Canada
www.pajamapress.ca

 MIX
Paper from
responsible sources
FSC   FSC® C004071
www.fsc.org

 ANCIENT FOREST ™
FRIENDLY

For my son, Colin

I'm puffing up the hill

     to Swiff Dunphy's place,
delivering a letter from our PO Box
that should've gone in his.
                        Why me?
Because Roxy's studying World History at Kaitlin's—
and if you believe that, you'll believe
anything. Mom swallowed it whole. Like always.

Like always,
       Loren drifts into my head,
            her hair smooth as polished birch,
                  her fuzzy pink sweater in French class...

Smoke hangs low
over Swiff's roof, alders jab
the windowpanes.
Grass hasn't been scythed
in ten years.
       The dog—the dog looks
dead.
I freeze.
She blinks.

How do I know it's female?
It's lying down. No way to tell if
it's a squatter or a leg-lifter.

I walk closer.
Beaten mud crisscrossed by old planks. Chain stretching
from a metal post to the dog's collar.
                              Stunned eyes.

Wind freshens off the gulf. Waves grumble on the rocks.

Swiff swaggers onto the porch. "You're trespassin'."
I pass him the letter.
He reeks of booze and unwashed Swiff, veins tracking his nose
as if a kid went haywire with a red pen.
He squints at the envelope.
"From Arnie Bellweather. Buddy o' mine—
I used to fish with his ol' man. How come you got the letter?"

I shrug.

"My name's on it. My box number. Can't they read?"
                         He spits.
Misses my left boot by a nail-length.
"Got nothin' to say for yourself, kid? If you're waitin' for
a handout, you'll wait longer than a jig
                    for a twenty-pound cod."

He cackles at his own joke.

Dog's still lying there.

Loren Cody

has blond hair and blue eyes—which doesn't begin to describe her.

She's beautiful...like the end table Dad designed, its simple, clean lines
finished with linseed, so all you want to do is

run your fingers over it.

It's like there's a quietness to her. A dignity. Jeez, I'm talking BS.

She's going steady with Chase McCallum.
Seven and a half months.

Okay, let's get this out of the way—

fifteen years old and he's *puffing up the hill?*
What's with this guy?

From kindergarten
to grade seven
I got called Fatty Humbolt.

Fatty Humbolt
had boobs and love handles
and you had to poke to locate
wrists and ankles. All four cheeks fat.

Have more French fries, Nixon...another helping of battered fish...
more pork scraps...gravy...doughboys...

Then my growth spurt
started spreading the fat around.
I glimpsed
the possibility
of bones.

The cakes iced with love,
the pies bubbly with love,
the chicken stuffed with love,

and I said *no.*

Don't get me wrong—
I'm no Firefighter-of-the-Month.
But I'm still growing
and I've got cheekbones

and one chin, not two.
Yeah, I could lose
ten pounds
and athletic I'm not.
But, man,
compared to grade four—

Roxy rushes into the kitchen, mascara

in one hand,
in the other,
      bristled
hair brush
      aimed
at my chest.
Metal-studded bag
          slung
over her shoulder. Matching stud
in her left nostril
—and yeah,
         Modern Warfare
erupted the night she came home
with that.

Mom,
who's making our sandwiches,
gives Roxy
her cheery *isn't-it-a-lovely-day-dear* smile
that drives me into the middle of next week.
         Then
it registers. Roxy's wearing my Iron Maiden t-shirt.
The one that shrank
because Mom tossed it in the dryer
on High frigging Heat.

"Go take that off."
"Can't—we'll miss the bus."
"It's from their last tour!"

"It's too small for you. Mom, how often do I have to tell you—
        one slice of bread."
"But it's a souvenir."
"Souvenir? Suck it up, Nix,
        you've never seen them live."
"Rub it in, why don't you? And I wish you'd stay out of my room."
"Like you don't want a real human being in there?"
"Like you're the expert on humanity?"

"Now, Nixon," Mom says, "don't make such a fuss."

Mom never calls me Nix.

Roxy flicks my cheek with her fingernail. I hate it
when she does that. "The world's divided into winners
        and losers, little bro."
"I'm way taller than you!"
                Dammit,
why do I always sound five instead of fifteen
when I fight with my sister?

Mom frowns at the t-shirt.
"A skeleton in hockey gear with flames bursting out of his skull?"

Roxy and her one-slice sandwich head for the mudroom door.
"The skeleton has a name, Mom.
Eddie."

Mom sighs.
I pick up my lunch.
She says, absent-like, "Did you do your French homework, Nixon?
Grade nine is a very important year."
                "Oui, oui."

I flip my winter jacket off the hook—it's March,
                        wind like an auger.

I'd give ten t-shirts
to be ten rows back
at an Iron Maiden concert
right now.

Roxy and me stand
                          on opposite sides
of the driveway
waiting for the bus.

Bullbirds Cove
Gulf of St. Lawrence, Newfoundland

Houses cast up onshore
        like lobster traps.
Two skiffs and a longliner
moored in the lee
of the government wharf.

In front of our place, a dirt road and the landwash,
clatter of rocks rounded by the tides.
        Gizzard Island and Bullet Reef with their roughed-up surf.

The barrens are behind us, across the main highway.
        Mom used to take us there every summer,
                        blueberries pinging
in our pails, bakeapples with their saw-toothed leaves.

In the distance,
mountains planed by glaciers
in the last ice age.
Mountains with names—
        Sugar Loaf, Seven Days Work, and the Three Brides—
always the last to lose their snow.
        The codfish are gone from the sea. Groundfishing
closed years ago. *Should've closed it sooner*, says Uncle Mort,
but they wouldn't listen to us—our jigs, our nets,
        our wallets
                empty.
Used to be thirty-seven families
in Bullbirds Cove. Now we're
        down to twenty-three.

Mom's clearing the supper table.

Roxy's pulling on her boots.
"I'm going to Melanie's," she says, "to help her with algebra.
One look at x + y
and she freaks out."

Algebra? Hitching into town, more like.

"Where's Melanie's phone number?" Mom says,
consulting the list of Roxy's friends on the refrigerator,
eleven names in all.

I don't have a list.

"Fifth from the top," Roxy says.
"It's a school night—be home by ten, Roxanne, and call me
        before you leave Melanie's."
"Yeah, yeah."

I slide past them.
Mom doesn't ask
where I'm going
or when I'll be back.

The workshop

is across the yard. There's a sign over the door.

Bertram Humbolt: Fine Furniture

Dad's about to leave for St. Jerrold.
I ask if I can go with him.

At Home Hardware, Dad heads for Tools.
I hurry to Pets,
snatch a long black leash
and a box of Milk-Bones,
whip through the cash,
shove the stuff in my backpack,
find Dad near nails and bolts.

He's holding a band-saw blade, 6 TPI,
as he mulls over brass screws.
I tell him we're low on veneer pins.

The box of Milk-Bones digs into my back.

Before the moratorium

on the cod fishery, Dad built
dories, fish shacks, houses for the fishermen's families.

After the moratorium,
he worked shifts at Home Hardware,
made picnic tables,
porch swings,
and those eight-sided
garbage boxes.

But at night,
      night after night,
          alone
      in the workshop,
he taught himself
how to make furniture,

furniture that will be sat on or sat at
long after every fish in the ocean
has been netted, trapped, dragged, or harpooned.

Loren

steps out of the undergrowth,
     she's not wearing any—
BEEP BEEP BEEP BEEP
I fall out of bed, stumble across my room
into the hall. Bathroom straight ahead. Boxers
     pointing the way.
I wish I wouldn't dream about Loren, not
     that kind of—
Roxy steps out of her bedroom.
Plaid PJs. Neon tank top.
She glances down. "Dude. Chill."

Why did God invent sisters.

School's out

and I'm partways
up the hill
to Swiff's place.

I stop for a breather.

Finger the Milk-Bones
in my pocket.
Wind's from the north,
my fleece
useless as a drag net.

> All this for a dog
> that looks like the dregs
> of a rummage sale?

I didn't take the tags
off the leash yet.
Dad's going
to Home Hardware
tomorrow night.

*Full refund in fourteen days
upon presentation of receipt.*

Swiff's heaping garbage

into his rusty old truck.
Doesn't look as though the dog's moved
since the last time I was here.

Even though she's a big dog,
aggressive and *dominant*
don't come to mind.

"You trespassin' again, kid?"
"What's your dog's name?"
He spits. "It don't need no name."

"Can I take her for a walk?"
"Walk? The *dog*?" Swiff heaves another bag
into the back of the truck. "I ain't gonna pay you."
"I'm not asking for pay."
"You be sure to fix the chain back on—that's a valuable dog."

     She's a mutt.

I walk toward her and hunker down.
Her coat's peat-brown, wiry,
no shine to it. Tufts of hair over her eyes,
which are golden-brown.
I put a Milk-Bone near her paws.
She ignores it.

     Piles of shit
     at the far end of the chain's reach.
     Stink of sour pee.

Taking my time, I clip the leash to her collar
and unclip the chain, then back off,
                    tugging gently.
Ears flat, she scrabbles into the kennel.

Swiff leans out of the cab of his truck,
            sniggering.
"She's a homebody, that dog—
good luck shiftin' her."
                    The engine judders
and farts, rocks shoot from under the tires
and he's gone.

Ten minutes pass. Me tugging,
her resisting.
Finally, I sit down on one of the planks,
the leash loose,
                    and listen to the wind in the alders.

She wheezes in her sleep.

Ten more minutes creep by.
When I latch the chain back on, the links
rattle. She wakes with a start
and for a moment
her eyes meet mine.

I never saw
such sadness,
such hopelessness.

I'm loading the dishwasher,

which is Roxy's job, but she's skived off.
A car pulls up by the house. Uncle Mort
gives his usual five-note knock,
and plods
into the kitchen, Aunt Gerd trotting on his heels.

"Coral," she says to Mom as I jam another plate into the rack,
"what a lovely boy your Nix is. So helpful.
Good company for you besides."

Like I'm not here.

Uncle Mort says, "He don't give you one spit of trouble,"
and helps himself to a cookie off the table.

I fit the last four glasses onto the rack,
close the dishwasher, mumble, "Homework—see you,"
and run for the stairs.

Given that everyone along the shore

keeps track of second cousins
three times removed,
we don't have many relatives.
None on Mom's side.
She gets snappy if you question her.

Uncle Mort is Dad's only brother.
Their parents, Gramps and Gram,
died within two weeks of each other,
like their devotion couldn't be stretched
longer than fourteen days.

Dad inherited his morals from Gramps,
who belonged to a stony little sect
in the outport on Gizzard Island.

No
lying, stealing,
divorce, debts, drunkenness,
premarital sex,
or cribbage.
Always
be kind to your neighbors,
forgive your enemies,
and pay your taxes on time.

Now that Gramps is dead,
Dad plays a mean game of crib.
The rest?
Solid as a headstone.

BEEP BEEP BEEP

A whole day of school to look forward to
     and Roxy's filched the bathroom.
I can't wait for her to move out so I don't have to deal with
bubble bath and tampons.
I bang on the door.
"Five minutes!" she hollers.

Five means fifteen.
I pee downstairs.
Shovel in cereal and toast.

When I go back up, Roxy's coming out of the bathroom.
Double take.
"What do you think?" she says.
I grin at her. "Awesome."
"Vampire Red." She tosses her hair. "Brown is boring."
"Mom won't like it."
"Or Dad," she says.
"That why you did it?"
"Needed to jazz up my social life."
I run my fingers through my own hair.
Regular orange. "We clash."
"Not always—remember *two's tougher than one?*"

It's what we used to chant when we were young,
     me chubby and scared shitless
of Kendel Green. Back then, Roxy
was Roxanne to all of us, not just to Mom,
who still refuses to call her anything but Roxanne.

We go downstairs together.
Mom blathers on.
Dad looks pained.

Then we walk down the driveway,
Roxy smoothing her hair,
             me talking tough,
             trashing Kendel.

Roxanne

was going to save
polar bears up north,
junkies on Vancouver's Lower East Side,
the garbage people of Puerto Rico.
She was going to change her name
to Teresa, marry a rich man
and distribute alms—her word—to the poor.
I was going to be her assistant.

Somehow we never thought of saving
S-Stevie P-P-Poole,
who was a magnet for bullies.
Or Del Brewster's wife Angie,
whose face was often bruised
and always frightened.

Roxanne and me and Mom and Dad
used to play Skip-bo at the kitchen table.
Roxanne looked so innocent

and won every game.

When she was six
Roxanne loved finger paints.
Giant yellow suns with splashy rays
that made you happy,
and her trees—
huge green globes,
not like anything that grows in Bullbirds Cove.

She was always trying to get me
to color outside the lines.
And once or twice I did.

I thought the yellow sun
rose over the mountains and set over the sea
on my sister Roxanne.

Then she hit puberty.
Head-on collision.

She changed her name.

To Roxy.

The kitchen smells of roast chicken.

Mom's standing by the stove, tipping
frozen corn into a saucepan.
She smiles at me. "Hungry, Nixon?"
Her eyes are pretty, like birch leaves in spring.
Unlike mine. Sludge-green. Canned peas.
"Sorta hungry," I say.

You never want to underestimate
my mom. Joe Godsell, up the road,
keeps free-range hens. When they're done laying,
it's the chop
(yep, it's true, they stagger around headless
     before they
flump in a flurry of feathers.
I watched one day. Disgusting.)
     He hangs them
so the blood drips out, then plucks them. Mom
guts them. In the sink. Cheaper that way.
Bloated blue-gray twists of intestine,
the red-black liver and tough little heart.
Her face calm, she says Joe's hens taste better
than store-bought.

Roxy makes her usual entrance

after the three of us have sat down.
Dad's already carved the chicken.
She's wearing jeans and a top
that exposes the maximum cleavage
permitted by the school board. She's only
eleven months older than me.
Might as well be eleven years.

She drops into her chair. "Chicken
again?" she says. "Pass the potatoes, Dad."

Helping herself to a small scoop,
she says, "I have a date with Bryan Sykes
tomorrow night. Movie and a pizza."

Oh man.
Your drug of choice? Ask Bryan.
House parties where the empties
would fill a dump truck and the beds
are the busiest place in town? Ask Bryan.
And who's the sexiest guy
at St. Jerrold Consolidated? Just ask Bryan.

"Bryan Sykes?" Mom says. "The politician's son?"
"So?" Roxy says.
"That's nice for you, dear, that's all I meant.
Mr. Sykes had our road graded,
and he's done a lot for the St. Jerrold Hospital."

"Bryan's in grade twelve," I say. "Too old for you."

Mom sits up straight. "Grade twelve?"
"He's mature, Mom," Roxy says, "not like the jerks
in grade ten. He's been to Paris and Athens.
He'll expand my horizons."
"You've got that right," I say.
Roxy smiles at me, her killer-shark smile.
"He has a younger sister.
You should ask her out—Loren Cody's
never going to look your way."

I don't blush like ordinary people. My forehead
scorches. My ears blaze. How does she know about Loren?
I didn't think anyone did.

Mom switches her attention to me.
She only gets on my case is if she thinks
I'm gonna fail French
or
I'm within spitting distance of sex.
"Nixon, do you know Bryan's sister?"
I shake my head.

Vampire Red's to blame for all this.

Then Mom's back to Roxy. "Will Bryan be driving?
How long has he had his licence? Has he ever had an accident?"
"He has his own car," Roxy says
with a pointed look at Dad. "A Lexus.
His father gave it to him two years ago
when he turned sixteen."
"So he's eighteen? That's a big age difference when—"
"Dad's *ten* years older than you."

Dad says, "Don't sauce your mother.
No drinking, and I don't just mean tonight.

The same goes for you, Nix—
and Roxy, stay out of Bryan's car if he's been drinking.
Call me for a drive instead."

"Of course." Roxy lowers her lashes.
My sister is a pro at *demure*
when it comes to Dad.
She doesn't waste it
on Mom
or me.

In a real funk

(Mom must've put him up to it because of Bryan's sister)
Dad takes me by the elbow after supper
and tugs me into the den.
"You have these health classes in school, right?"

I nod.
"So you know what's what."
I nod again. Outright lie. How can you know until

you buy the condom,
haul the condom on,
and put it where it's supposed to go?
"Good," says Dad.

You can almost see him wipe his brow.

Then he says, "Nix, you'd know if Roxy took a drink?"
"Guess so."
"She's not steady like you. She bears watching."

So that's *my* job?

"We worry about her," Dad says. "Good to know
you're on our side, Son."
He claps me on the shoulder,
man to man,
and leaves the den.

Dad's not a believer in fathers hugging sons.
When a goal's scored in the NHL, that's when guys hug guys.

Roxy flings

my door open, steps inside
and bangs it shut.
        Me in my boxers
because I'm changing into my old duds.
I drag a t-shirt that smells of sawdust
over my head. "You ever think of knocking?"

She looks me up and down. "You know, you're not
half-bad. If you got rid of a few zits
and the flab around your waist...oh yeah, and did something
about your hair."

No matter what I do, my hair
won't lie flat. A cowlick is called a cowlick
because your hair looks like a Holstein scoured it with her tongue.

Roxy prods me in the chest.
"Me and Bryan? Back off."

"He's a badass, Rox. Outta your league."
"I know the score."

Giving unwanted advice to my older sister
isn't one of my life skills, but gimme credit
for trying. "Bryan will put the moves on you."

She smirks. "Your point is?"
"Not *that* kind of move. Remember Lyall Brewster?
Lost several million brain cells
        from crap in the hash Bryan sold him."
"I'm smarter than Lyall ever was."

"If you're halfways smart
you'll stay away from Bryan Sykes!"
She shoves her face at mine.
Although I'm four inches taller,
I step back.
             "Don't say one more word
to Mom and Dad about Bryan. Or I'll tell Chase
how you drool over Loren."

Roxy's never been a back-stabber—
slices you in the belly
and smiles while you bleed.

Three years ago—in my Fatty Humbolt days—

Chase stopped two guys
        who were punching on me
behind the school bus, and ever since
he smiles at me and sometimes sits with me
in the cafeteria, which is enough to keep the jocks
off my back. But
you wouldn't exactly call him
a friend.
        Why would Chase McCallum—
top-scorer in the Western AAA—
put up with a slug like me?

And why would his girlfriend even notice I exist?

I stomp to the workshop, unlock the deadbolt
and switch on the lights.
Whiff of sawdust and epoxy.
        Gleam of tung oil
        on the Windsor chair Dad designed.
Band-saw squat on the concrete floor.

I'm working on a cherry wood side table,
        a surprise for Mom's fortieth.
I pick up the back rail where I cut the tenons the other night,
take a deep breath,
and clear my mind.
Coping saw to remove the waste.
Beveled chisel to clean up the edges.
Ditto for the other end of the back rail
and both side rails. Next,

miter the tenons and test the fit.
After a few passes of 240-grit, it's perfect.
Always quit while you're ahead.

I picture the table in the front hall,
wax making the wood glow.

Dad.

Your first cut is on the waste side of the line.

Never use the table saw.

Keep your chisels sharp enough to slice the hairs on your arm.

The scars on my knuckles?
From Dad's chisels.

When the blade nicked my thumb
instead of a walnut coat rack,
Dad said, sober as the tax man, "Blood's
a poor man's varnish."

Only time I ever heard him joke.

I'm rooting in my locker

for my French scribbler, which I swear goes missing on purpose,
when behind me Chase says, "Hey, Nix."

I straighten. "Hey."
"You around this weekend?"

I nod.

He's standing there, half-smile on his face.

C'mon, Nix, say something. "You playing tomorrow night?"

"House league, in St. Jerrold.
Scoters vs Codroy Cougars. You going?"
"Maybe."
"My sister's been getting on my case—she has a project for you.
Can I bring her to your place in the morning?"

"Guess so."
"Around eleven?"
"I'll be in the workshop."

He shoulder-jabs me and walks away.

I find the scribbler

under a pile of binders.
I'm digging through my pack for a pen
when Kendel Green
                hip-checks me
                into my locker,
                the edge a blunt axe.

"Hey there, Fatty," he says, big grin
like we're best buddies.

      He attracts girls
      same way
      the dump attracts gulls.

One of these days
I'll go for his throat.

He keeps walking. I bend to pick up the papers
that spilled out of my pack. Why don't I
kick 'em across the corridor?
      Then Roxy's crouching beside me.
Her fingernails are turquoise,
decorated with white butterflies.
"Kendel's an asshole, bro—
recommended career path
           Ultimate Fighting."
She passes me the last of the papers. "I'm late
for World History. War will break out
between me and Ms. Crouse. Take notes."

The big date with Bryan is tonight.
That's why she's in a good mood.

* * *

At noon, our homeroom teacher
deals out report cards
in their pale gray envelopes,
parent's signature required.

In Eng-lish class, Ham-let is mouth-ing off.

Last period, I sweat oral French.
Non, je n'ai pas étudié les mots vocabulaires.

Final touch? When I toil up the hill to Swiff's,
the damned dog
ignores me.

I place my midterm Report Card on the supper table next to Mom's fork.

Nixon refuses to speak up in class.	–Science
Please—more classroom participation!	–French
Learning to express himself verbally would be to Nixon's advantage.	–Social Studies
Reticent.	–English
Unless he addresses his issues around communication, Nixon will be unsuited for any occupation that requires interfacing with the public.	–Guidance Counsellor

The first time
I came across the word
introversion
was the first time
I recognized myself. Like,
there was a category
for me.

I spend thirty hours a week
in school,
where *extroversion*
is the only version.

Dad reads the report card first,
then passes it to Mom,
        shaking his head.
Mom reads it, frowning. "Really, Nixon—
if you don't learn to speak up for yourself, all you'll get
is some dead-end job for the rest of your life.
Is *that* what you want?"

Sure, Mom, that's exactly what I want.

For her first date with Bryan,

Roxy's wearing jeans (low-cut, skin-tight),
a sweater (low-cut, tighter than skin),
and a pink diamond in her belly button.

Mom goes ballistic. "You're not leaving the house
looking like that. Upstairs this minute and change your clothes."
"I'll be late!"
"If you dress for trouble, Roxanne, you'll find it.
And wipe off some of that eye shadow."
"Mom, I'm *sixteen*."
"Obey your mother," Dad says.

Roxy clomps up the stairs, comes down
                            in a purple sweater, XL.
I'd bet my latest version of Modern Warfare
the sweater will be dumped
before she's in the Lexus.

"Much better," Mom says. "Have a nice time, dear."

                    * * *

When Roxy comes home, three minutes
before midnight, I casually walk down the stairs
as she sways up them.
      Second-hand smoke,
      whiff of expensive aftershave,
      not a hint of booze.
But her smile—
because, yeah, she smiles at me—
it's too...soft.

Roxy doesn't do *happy*.

"How'd the date go?" I say.
She grinds her hips like she's on a dance floor. "He is sooo
totally hot."
"You didn't—"
why don't I just shut up
when I know damn well she did?
"Cool it, bro. I'm sixteen years old—isn't it about time?
I sure wouldn't want anyone at school to know I waited this long."
She sends another smile my way.
A smile like one of her yellow suns.
"He was worth waiting for—believe me."

Yesterday evening, to keep my mind off

Bryan, drugs, and drink,
I cut mortises and tapered the table legs.
This morning, it's dovetails
in the front rail, step by step,
            slow and careful.
Then I start the leg sockets.
I'm scribing the end grain when

                someone knocks on the door.
The knife
misses my finger
by ⅛". Chase
and his sister. *Oh shit.*
"Come in."

Chase grins at me. "Hey, Nix...you know Blue."

Blue McCallum is in grade eight.
Same school as me because they closed the junior high.

Just because we travel the same bus
doesn't mean we know each other.

She's fourteen, tall,
baggy down jacket, baggy jeans,
black hair scraped into a skimpy braid.

Her eyes *are* blue, dark blue,
like the paint on Dad's truck.

She looks around with interest.

"Can you work all this stuff?"
I nod.
"Will you make me four birdhouses? Real ones,
not like the ones you sold at the craft fair."
"Jeesh," Chase says, "insult the guy,
        why don't you?"
Although she glares at him, she's blushing.
"They were cool, Nix,"
she says. "But I need good drainage
and one side hinged
so I can clean the box.
Feces."
"Oh," I say.
"And lice."

She passes me a book. "The plans are on page forty.
Two for chickadees and two for tree swallows."

I try to act professional. "White cedar or pine?"
"Up to you."

She might look like a stray,
but she behaves like Chase—
                confident.
Their dad, a plumber, is the champion fiddler
from St. Anthony to Port aux Basques.
Their mom makes quilts out of colors that skin your eyes.

After we've settled time and price, Chase picks up
a front rail. "Is this part of the table?"
"Yeah."
"What's this angled bit?"
"Shoulder."
"Nix," he says, "I'm asking because I want to know."

When I try to describe where I'm at
with the joints, the words tangle
my tongue. So I pick up the dovetail saw,
cut into the sockets, chisel out the waste,
and fit the rail into the leg.
Other side the same,
and by now I've forgotten
anyone's watching. Screw slots next,
counter-sinking the holes.
                    As I lay down the drill,
Blue says, "You don't need words.
Your hands
do the talking."
                    I gape at her. "Huh?"
Chase laughs. "You've nailed him, Blue!"

Blue smiles at me. "Thanks, Nix.
Let me know when the birdhouses are ready."
"See you," Chase says,
and they're out the door.

Lice

        ricocheting inside my birdhouses,
feces on the floor. If I wanted to build
pigpens, I would.

So Blue's gonna pay me. Big frigging deal.

I take pride in my work.
        If a bird crapped on Dad's furniture—
you wouldn't want to be anywhere near him.

Then there's Chase.
He asked a straightforward question.
Do I answer?
Nah. I pick up a chisel and a chunk of wood.

A dumb-assed carpenter,
that's what Blue saw.

Is that what Loren sees?

The dog's lying on the frozen mud.

Swiff's on the front porch. "You back, kid?"
"You ever let your dog in the house?"
"In the *house?* She's a guard dog, not one o' them
                                        dinky Chihuahuas."
"Only thing to guard around here is dog shit."
"The kennel's her place. She knows it
and so do I."
            He spits over the railing
and disappears inside.

I walk toward the kennel. Her dark brown coat,
her skinny legs and tail, and my brain makes that leap
our English teacher raves on about.
                                        "I'll call you Twig."

No ears perked up, no tail wagging.
Twig doesn't do dogspeak
anymore than I do chitchat.

We go through the leash-tug-resist routine.

I plunk my butt on the plank nearest her.
"You could be walking the barrens. Foxes out there,
and rabbits. Better smells than you're used to."

Is she even listening? I balance a biscuit
                        on her paw
and tell her about Bryan Sykes
and Mom's table. As I'm repeating
Dad's one and only joke,

Twig nudges the Milk-Bone, tilts her head
as it falls on the mud, picks it up
                                        delicate-like,
and crunches it into little pieces. Then
she licks her lips, puts her head down,
and shuts her eyes.

Leash off.
Chain on.
Back down the hill
feeling like I just won
the full discount
on *Scratch and Save.*

Dad drives me to the rink,

a first for both of us, hockey
not being on my radar.

He stops in the parking lot
to talk to Uncle Mort and Aunt Gerd,
who volunteer in the canteen twice a week.
I wave at them and hurry inside.

The arena—home of the St. Jerrold Scoters—was built a year ago.
          The air's cold, trapped,
not like the wind off the gulf on a February morning.

The teams are already on the ice.
                            Loren
is standing by the rail with her friends.

I stride past, eyes front, and sit by myself
at the far end of the arena.

        MCCALLUM flashes by
on the back of a white jersey. So white jerseys are Scoters
and black are Cougars. Makes me feel sorta smug,
knowing which team is which.

The game starts.
A girl says, "Hi," and sits down beside me.
A girl in a baggy down jacket.
Blue.
Not Loren.
Why would I

even for a split second
think it would be Loren?

Two minutes in, a ref leads a Scoter
out the gate. I must look confused
because Blue says, "Checking from behind—
he'll be sent to the dressing room."
Next penalty is for high-sticking. Players bounce
        off each other,
                                thud
against the boards. Then
a burly guy from the other team
ploughs into Chase
                                knocking him
clean off his feet. His helmet
                                whacks
                                the ice.
The crowd boos.

Blue mutters, "They're trying to take him out.
He's our best player."
Chase levers himself off the ice and reaches
for his stick. Bends double,

stays that way too long.
Blue's fingers twist in her lap. "I'm always scared
he'll get hurt. But it's like I can't stay away."

No point saying he'll be fine,
not the way these guys are ripping up the rink.
Final score:
        4-2 for the Scoters,
three of those goals Chase's.

Hockey moms blow air horns and clash
tambourines. The teams that five minutes ago
were doing their best to kill each other
shake hands.

Blue says, "Want a drive home?"
"No." The word out so fast I blink.
Chase will be driving Blue home,
Loren in the front seat beside him.

"I only offered you a drive to be polite!
I'm more interested in birds than boys."

Even fluorescent lights can't make Blue's eyes
anything but deep blue—
real deep blue, because she's pissed off.

She turns her back and walks away.

The hill to Swiff's place

is a killer.
                              Crows yakking
in the spruce trees. Purple clouds over the mountains—
Sugar Loaf, Seven Days Work,
and the Three Brides.
                              Yesterday
Twig wolfed three Milk-Bones. Today,
          when she sees me coming,
she raises her head. One ear up, one down.

Swiff yells, "Stay where yer at, dog!"
Her head drops to her paws.
"Swiff, quit interfering!"
"Lippy, ain't ya?"
He shambles inside, and the door bangs shut.

Not often I get called *lippy*.

I clip on the leash. "Twig, let's prove him wrong.
C'mon, it's a sunny day and the snow's thawing."

Milk-Bone on her paw. Chomp. Swallow.
Milk-Bone on the mud
                              just beyond her reach.
She hesitates, grabs,
and gulps it down.
          Milk-Bone two feet farther away.
She gives me a look. *I know what you're up to.*

I back up, the leash loose.

Two Milk-Bones later, we're into the grass, its long tufts
sticking through the snow. She sniffs,
                    cautious,
then buries her face in some dry stalks.

Three more Milk-Bones
bring us to the dirt road.

She sits down.
I beg.
I coax.
I plead.
She won't budge.

My homework,

including French, has been lying in wait ever since I got off the bus.
I lay out textbooks, sharpen four pencils, open my binder,
add more looseleaf.
Go downstairs and pour a glass of apple juice.
Carry it upstairs.
Close the door.
Sigh.
Decide Iron Maiden might get me moving.
Look for my smartphone.
Can't find it.

I march across the hall, bang on Roxy's door.
"Go away!"
I knee the door open.
She's sitting on the bed, pillows heaped behind her,
my phone on the blanket,
her nose in a book. On the cover,
a dragon, a red-ringed moon, and a girl with bloodshot eyes.

"Gimme my phone," I say.
"Later," she says and turns the page.
"Where's yours?"
"I left it in school."
"I'm gonna put a lock on my door if you don't quit
going in my room!"

"Tell you what," she says, pulling out the earbuds,
"I'll give the phone back if you'll put a lock on *my* door."
"You're asking *me* to do *you* a favor?"
She dangles the cord from her finger. "No lock, no phone."

"Okay, okay!"

"Great," she says. "That way, Mom can't come in here.

BTW, you have rotten taste in music.

'Bring Your Daughter to the Slaughter'?

Jeez, Nix, you're a waste of space."

The stuffed polar bear Mom gave her

sits at the end of Roxy's bed.
His name was Fierce.
But when she wrote a story about him in grade four,
she spelled it f-e-a-r-c-e, and he's been
Fearce ever since.
                    Why do I chicken out
When Roxy gets in my face? And why am I so afraid
of guys like Kendel? Last six months
I've been taller than him.

Fear to fierce.
How do you *do* that?

Here's what I didn't see in Roxy's room:

For her sixteenth birthday, I made her
a jewelry box. Maple and walnut,
8˝ x 8˝
with mitered corners
and a narrow rabbet on the lid,
the walnut waxed to a rich, dark sheen.
I lined it with green felt.

She liked it. I could tell.

Haven't seen it since.
Likely it's hidden in the back corner of her closet.
On the floor.
Under a pile of dirty socks.

I play Modern Warfare

on Xbox, campaigning
with the U.S. Marine Corps.
Our mission: take out an informer.
My weapon: MP5. Palm trees,
barbed wire, a line of wash
hanging limp. Blood
spattered on a concrete wall.
My night-vision goggles
turn everything green.
      Then I get hurt.
The screen flares
red and I hear myself
groan. Soldiers yelling orders,
a truck's on fire—*shit*,
I'm killed by a grenade.
Back to the last checkpoint.
Respawn.

The radio says forty percent chance

of showers or flurries. Out the window
it's pissing down rain. Sea
a pock-marked gray. Loppy
waves. In slicker and boots
I trudge up the hill. No sign

of Swiff. When I whistle,
Twig trots out of the kennel,
her scraggly tail waving.
I grin like a lunatic.
We amble through the grass to the road.
I throw a Milk-Bone to the far side
                of the ditch.
"Okay, Twig,
now or never."

She jumps the ditch so fast
I'm nearly jerked off my feet,
and we're off, strutting
down the road like we do this
every day.

We cross the highway
and take the first trail
onto the barrens,
where juniper and tamarack
shore up the snow
between patches of soggy peat.
Twig darts from here
                to there,

gulping smells
as if they're Milk-Bones,

me staggering
through slush and mud.
Sugar Loaf swallowed by the rain.
Seams of my slicker
definitely not waterproof.
Long time since I felt this good.

I should've known she'd get on my case.

"Do you have a girlfriend?" Mom says. "Is that where you go
every afternoon? Is it Bryan's younger sister,
the one Roxanne mentioned?
I know you and your father had another talk,
but you mustn't ever—"

"Mom, I'm walking Swiff Dunphy's dog."

She spills flour on the counter.
I snag an oatmeal cookie and bolt for the stairs.

Roxy brings Bryan to the house

Friday night, to meet Mom and Dad.

He's tall
with a classy haircut
and Hollywood-slick good looks.
Long-sleeved YSL shirt, his watch
with enough dials to fly a jumbo jet.

He's also stone-cold sober.
His pupils regular size.

And Roxy? With a jolt—like I've never seen my sister before—
it's movie stars that are supposed to be *radiant*,
not girls from Bullbirds Cove.

She introduces Bryan
to Mom and Dad.
He calls them Mr. and Mrs. Humbolt
then calls Dad *sir*.
Mom says, with her prettiest smile,
"This is our son, Nixon."
"Nixon," he says,
his hand scrunching mine.
"Nix," I say, face in scowl-mode.
His smile doesn't falter. Staple-gun eyes.
They all stand around
making polite conversation.
Enough to make you barf.
             Easy to see
Mom's fallen for him. Dad—

you never know what he's thinking
because he never
says.

But the way Bryan looks at Roxy—protective,
caring, respectful—can that be fake?

I'm knackered—

tripped and fell flat in a bog, Twig puzzled
to see my face
                lower than hers.

I trail up the driveway,
wondering if this is how Chase feels
after every hockey game.

Inside, Roxy's smiling at her phone
like she just won a cruise to the Caribbean.
Only one person puts that yellow-sun smile
on her face.
                She checks out my dirty slicker

and winks at me. "Did you lie down
so Loren Cody could walk all over you?
Or were you having it off with her behind the arena?"
"Shut up!"
"Confess, Nix."

I say sulkily, "Every afternoon, I walk
Swiff Dunphy's dog."

"No kidding? What for?"
She looks interested. Like, very.
I shrug—guaranteed to set her off.

She says, "You're trying to lose the flab over your gut."
I shrug again.
"You're getting in shape for the summer sports program."
I don't even bother to shrug.

Two little chisel-marks gouge her forehead.
"Don't give me *strong and silent*!
                              Safe and silent,
that's your gig. *Let's play with nails,*
let's avoid all sports, let's fall for a girl
who belongs to someone else—remember
the box you made for my birthday?
That's how you live your life, inside
a box you've made yourself."
"I don't!"
"Think about it." One last shot. "And
where's the lock for my door?"

Final score? Roxy 1: Nix 0.

You'd think by now
I'd know better.
And I do *not*
live my life inside a box.

I wait two days

then I Google prices of doorknobs with locks,
all the brands Home Hardware carries.

I print them off.
Slide them under Roxy's door.
She picks one. Fast.

"Money up front," I say. "Including tax."
She bitches. But she forks it over.

I kinda forget to go with Dad to Home Hardware.
Twice.
Figure that's the limit.

I buy new doorknobs complete with lock
and two keys, Antique Nickel. Dad's scut work—
my responsibility—suddenly takes priority.
"Serious backlog," I tell her, real serious.
She bitches some more.

From long experience, I know just how far
I can push my luck.
Two hours before she'll blow her stack,
I gather my tools—
             Oops, forgot the drill...
             and what did I do
             with the screws? Roxy, you seen the screws?
—and neatly replace the old doorknobs
with the new ones. With a flourish,
I pass her one of the keys.

She shuts the door in my face.
The lock clicks.

All evening,
        on her stereo,
top volume,

she plays D.O.A.,
The Gaslight Anthem,
and Deadmau5.

For over a week

the high temperatures have broken all the records
for early April.
                Blackflies
thirsty for blood.
Snow rotting in the hollows.
I use *Off!*
teach Twig *Come!*
Sit!
I still don't dare let her off the leash
in case her paws taste freedom and never stop running.

She's filling out and frisky.
I'm losing flab.
Muscles—actual muscles—
in my calves,
and if I poke my thighs,
they're, like, hard.

                             * * *

One Saturday, when we're a long ways
out there,
      I collapse on a rock
and Twig lays her head on my knee
and gazes up at me,
and if that's not love shining from her eyes
there's no granite under my butt.
"Me too," I whisper,
scratching her head until she's bleary-eyed.

The silence of the barrens
presses on my ears, as old and solid
as the mountains.
    "Sometimes,"
I say, "I wish I was more like Chase—
the way he can talk to anyone. 'Think outside the box,'
that's what our math teacher says—
I don't even talk outside the box.
It's like silence is my job."

Twig gives me one of her looks.
    Your job?
    Dogshit.

We're straggling home, me squashing

blackflies

     on my neck,

           ears,

forehead,

       wrists,

when I catch sight of Blue.
She's staring through a pair of binocs
at the top of a spruce tree
as though a whole host of angels just landed.

Far as I can see, it's one measly bird.

Twig runs up to her. The bird flies away.
Blue turns, sees me.
"You just scared off the first fox sparrow
I've seen this year. You and your dog."

"Oh. Sorry. Her name's Twig."

"Twig? For a dog the size of a small tree?"
"Kinda scrawny tree."

Blue's smile breaks through, a smile
that doesn't hold anything back.
Trustworthy. Which is a funny way to describe—
"Is there peanut butter on my teeth?" she says.
"Huh? No!"
"I ate a sandwich a few minutes ago. Want some fly dope?"
"Too late."

She laughs and reaches up,
        her fingers
lightly slapping my throat.
"They sure like you."

The blush starts at my blood-smeared collar.
A notebook's stuck in one front pocket
of her shirt, a pen in the other. Under them
she's got great—under my jeans I'm—
Blue swats a bug on my ear
        my face so hot
        it'll barbecue
        the frigging blackflies.

I lower my eyes.
        Say something.
        Anything.
"How'd you get that big scratch on your arm?"
"I was watching a kittiwake and tripped over a rock."
"Shit, Blue, you should be careful. Anyone know
you come out here alone?"

She tilts her head. "Anyone know *you* come out here alone?"

"Guess not. I better go,
French quiz tomorrow. See ya."

She gives me another of those smiles.
I look anywhere but at her shirt.
It's Loren I'm in love with.

I call Twig and take off
like the morality squad's after me.

Swiff's on the porch

when we get back. He stares at Twig
like, *this is my dog?*
                              Spooks me.
Between a puff of blue smoke and a splat
                                        of spit,
he says slowly, "She looks good."

He's not mean to Twig. He's just
half-arsed
stem to stern.

Twig on the barrens is 100 percent dog—
from her whiskers
to the tip
of her scraggly tail.
But in Swiff's kennel?
Nowheres near.

Only place I'm 100 percent
is in the workshop.

I'm trying to decide

whether I want apple juice (healthy)
or Dr. Pepper (not).
Behind me, a girl says, "Silly bitch,"
with as much feeling as if she's saying
it's gonna rain tomorrow. "She just doesn't get it—
his absolute max is a month, and it's already
more than three weeks."
"Not that you're counting," says a second girl.
I search through my pocket, take out some coins.

"Who isn't counting? Bryan's the cutest guy
from here to St. Anthony."
"I wish to God she'd quit acting like she's on *American Idol*."
"Or like she's one of us. A senior."
"*Big* mistake."
"He'll drop her soon enough—Hey, buddy,
you gonna take all day making up your mind?"

I push the button.
Dr. Pepper.

In the cafeteria, I find a table to myself,

chow down on my egg-salad sandwich,
and play poker on my phone.
The two girls
were Lara O'Neill and Suzie Connor,
both in grade twelve.

Maybe they recognized me and figured
I'd pass the message to Roxy—
                              who, right now,
is at Bryan's table at the far side of the cafeteria,
acting like the life of the party.

Unless you're suicidal, stoned, or schizo,
you don't mess with
the St. Jerrold Consolidated Hierarchy.

Then—make my day—Kendel Green
stops at my table. "Hey, Fatty—
saw your sister hitching a ride into town
the other night.
              She still screwing Bryan Sykes?"
I'm on my feet, fists bunched and, yeah, I'm taller than him.
Kendel plants his hands
square on my chest,
              pushes hard. Off-
       balance,
I grab for the back
of the chair.
The chair crashes
into the next table.

The table leg squawks on the tiles.
A girl shrieks.
Heads turn.
I want to crawl under the table.
If you can die of humiliation, let it happen
soon.
          Kendel drawls, "Your sister
could teach you a thing or two,
seeing as you're a prize dork."

I clang the chair
back on its feet.
His big paws on my shoulders, Kendel
shoves me down on it—how come
he's so damn *strong*—and holds out his BlackBerry.
"Listen up. Text message—
          nix humbolt
          hot date Friday nite
Wanna know
who with, Nix? C'mon, guess."

Couple of guys snigger. My neck glows
like the elements on Mom's new stove.

"Clue in," Kendel says. "Mercy Bagley."
The sniggers turn to guffaws.
Mercy Bagley and her parents got born again,
and Mercy wears long black dresses
and tells us we're all on the high road
                              to Hell.
"Losers Incorporated," says Kendel.
"Where you taking her? Behind the arena?
Sure you know how to do the big It, buddy?
Want lessons from a pro?"

He knuckles the side of my head.
If I could find my tongue, I'd toss off
    a smart-ass one-liner.
If I had any balls, I'd flatten him.

If...if...if...
        Wherever I go,
Fatty Humbolt goes with me,
lugging boobs and love handles.

Behind me, Chase says,
"Kendel, we all know you're a stud
because you keep telling us.
Why don't you just move along?"

Hockey's number one at our school
and so's Chase, high-scorer in AAA.
    Kendel gives me
a friendly bash on the shoulder and saunters off.
Chase sits down. "Hey, Nix."

I wipe egg salad off my chin.

I almost stay home from the rink

even though I know Kendel isn't a big fan.
The sound of the chair crashing into the table—
it's been echoing in my head
                    ever since.
But this is the house league playoffs
and I owe Chase.
I follow some grade-seven kids through the door.

Uncle Mort and Aunt Gerd aren't on duty
in the canteen tonight. One less hassle.

Loren's wearing her pink jacket, her hair
so long and silky.... She smiles at me.
My heart
            skitters
        in my chest
like a chainsaw hitting a knot.

Blue's standing there, staring at me as if she knows
every secret I ever had. My face flares red.

She hesitates
before she walks over. "What's the word on the birdhouses?"
"I'll finish the table by the weekend. Then I'll start them."

Chase catches sight of her, waves his stick at both of us.
"Blue, d'you want to sit together?" I say,
and it comes out almost natural,
even though I can't believe I just said it.

She hesitates again.

Her smile—it's like...shy.
Blue McCallum? *Shy?*
"Okay," she says.

I wriggle my shoulders.
We sit down.
I try to pay attention
as she explains the difference between
back-checking
and checking-from-behind.

She doesn't ask if I want a drive home.

On my way out,

because I'm kinda chuffed that I asked a girl
to sit with me at the rink—even if she wasn't
the right girl—I take the wrong corridor
and end up by a door that's partways open.
Bryan Sykes and his sidekick
Cyril Watson, linebacker
on our less-than-amazing football team,
have weedy Lyall Brewster
backed against the wall.
Lyall's jeans aren't ripped as a fashion statement,
they're just ripped.
Cyril's big fist
is tugging Lyall by the hair
so the poor bugger's on tiptoes.
Cyril's big grin
shows he's enjoying himself.

"Cash up front, dude," Bryan says.
"I ain't got—"
"You want Cyril to break your fingers?"
Lyall turns pasty white.
Bryan leans forward, twists Lyall's nose.
Lyall bleats.
"Behind the arena," Bryan says. "Tomorrow,
nine p.m. Not a good idea
to keep us waiting."

He straightens.
Cyril lets go of Lyall's hair.

I beat a retreat, hiding behind
three sweat-soaked
hockey players who'll know
the way out.
          Near the exit
there's a security guard chatting up two girls.
Checking the corridors—guess it isn't in his job description.

* * *

If you want to catch Roxy
not chatting on her cell,
not texting,
and out of earshot of Mom and Dad,
you gotta be patient.
It doesn't happen until we're waiting for the bus the next morning.

I talk fast. "Bryan uses an enforcer for drug debts."
"Oh sure."
"Cyril Watson."
Her lashes flicker. "So Bryan deals," she says. "So what?
          He never uses."
"And that makes it okay?"
"All druggies are brain-dead—and that's one thing Bryan isn't!"
"Cyril's gonna break Lyall Brewster's fingers."
Her voice hardens. "I wish you wouldn't do this."
"You're the one who's brain-dead!"
"You know what?" she says, like she just figured out
the origins of the universe. "You're envious of Bryan."
"Huh? Envious of a creep
          who bleeds cash from the likes of Lyall?"
"You're not sexy.
You're not popular.
Of course you envy him!"

The look on her face—I've never been any good
at bucking that look.

* * *

Lyall must've come up with the money,
because in the cafeteria at noon
he has all his fingers.

Not a hope Roxy'll believe me now.

All the hours I've been putting into Mom's table

are clamped to my shoulders,
making my hands clumsy. What if the chisel slips
or the drill

        goes too deep?

I've glued the top, planed it, scraped it
until the metal was so hot
I burned my thumbs.
Okay,
so Dad cut the top to size
and supervised the router.
But
I'm the one who makes the joints and grooves
for the drawer.
        Which, dammit,
doesn't quite fit the carcass—
fancy word us woodworkers use
for the frame.
        More planing.
Drill a hole for the knob.
Drill pilot holes in the table top.
Screw the frame to the top.
Turn the whole thing
right way up
        and I've made a table.

Dad runs his fingertips over the top,
opens the drawer, and inspects the dovetails.

He smiles at me. "Nice work, Nix."

* * *

Sunday evening,
when I'm rubbing in the second coat of linseed,
Chase comes and watches.
He talks about the playoffs
and the prize his mom won at a Toronto art gallery
for one of her quilts.
I want to ask, *How's Loren?*

                    Tongue's
                    in a vise.

I'm watching an NHL game

with Dad. House league is a kids' tea party
compared to this. At 11:47
Roxy texts me.
>   *no drive home*
>   *no money for cab*

Bryan's doing a drug deal.
Bryan's polluted.
Bryan can't be bothered pushing the Start Button
on his shiny black Lexus.

"Dad, can you give Roxy a drive home?"
The announcer raises his voice and the crowd groans.
"Where is she?" Dad says. "She left it kinda late."

* * *

I go with him to St. Jerrold, to a big brick house
in the new subdivision.
A line of cars and trucks parked outside.
No Lexus.

Roxy comes down the path at a fast clip,
eyes front, shoulders tight.
"Thanks, Dad," she says, darts into the back seat,
snaps the door shut, jams her seatbelt into the socket,
crosses her arms over her chest, and ignores me.

>   Oh man. Either Bryan didn't come to the party
>   or he left without Roxy.

He's been dating her over a month—
over his limit, according to the girls in the cafeteria—

he better not mess with my sister.

Unless he already has.

Blue's blue eyes

light on the birdhouses.
She inspects the first one.
Dull brown preservative,
brass screws, drip lines,
and ventilation holes.
Who knew chickadees had
such complicated needs?
As I wait for the verdict, I'm
edgy as Twig when the wind blows
rabbit across the barrens.

Blue picks up another one. Chase says
in that lazy way of his, "Remember the day
we watched you make sockets for your table?
You were in the zone, man.
I've been thinking about it since—like, every hockey game
there's fans yelling, guys cursing, the *whump*
when you're blocked. But when the puck comes at you
and you see a gap, it's like everything else
              clicks off.
Sometimes the puck
flicks in the net
so clean, so sweet...
for the perfect shot, you gotta have that focus.
Most people wouldn't have a clue what I mean—
              but you do, Nix."
"Yeah."

He cuffs me on the side of the head.

I snap my fist to his gut and we're laughing.
Blue rolls her eyes.
Then she grins at me.
"The birdhouses are great," she says, "exactly what I wanted."

Chase says—same lazy voice—
"You ever make boxes? Small ones?"
I nod.
"I'd like to give Loren a box for her shells and sea-glass.
Quote me a price. Cash on delivery."

My brain stuttered to a halt
when he said *Loren.*
Is this how S-Stevie P-P-Poole feels
all the time?

Chase picks up my steel ruler.
"How about ten inches square, four inches deep?"

"Okay," I croak.
Blue's watching me.
To hell with her.

I'll make the most beautiful box in the world.

On Mom's fortieth

I uncover the table, the simple lines
and smooth edges I'm so proud of.
The wood glossy under the light.

Mom gazes at the table. Dismay
flares in her eyes.
Or is it horror?
Horror?
      She says in a voice like cracked
glass, "Nixon, it's lovely."
                Dismay
is nowheres near
what I'm feeling. I gabble,
"I made it for you. It's for the front hall.
It's cherry wood, a Shaker design.
You can keep your keys in the drawer.
The drawer has dovetails."

She's gripping Dad's arm,
her knuckles white. He says,
"What's wrong, Coral?"
                "Nothing!"
She gives me a hug so brief it's an insult.
"We'd better go. We don't want to be late
for dinner."

She loved Roxy's makeup kit
(special order from Halifax).
She loved Dad's card inviting her
to fly to St. John's and spend the weekend with him.

Blue liked the stupid birdhouses
more than Mom likes the table.

Next morning, the table's gone

from the front hall.
I stare at the blank wall as though staring
will order up a Shaker table
made from cherry wood.

It's in the living room,
covered with a flowered cloth so you can't see
the drawer with its polished knob.
A crystal vase sits on the cloth.

I'm in the kitchen with no memory
of how I got here.
"Mom, why don't you just tell me
you hate the goddamn table and be done with it?"

"Don't swear, Nixon!"
The timer dings.
She turns away, takes a pan of muffins
out of the oven. "It might get marked up in the front hall.
I wouldn't want anything to happen to it."
"But—"
"My favourite vase is on top," she says, as though that clinches it.
"But the table has—"
"Don't worry. When we have company, I'll show it off."
"It has four coats of linseed and one of wax. It won't— "
"Now, Nixon," she says—so calm, so damned reasonable—
"whose table is it?"

"Stuff's to be used, Mom!
If it's damaged, I can fix it."

Something splinters behind her eyes.
She tests a muffin with the tip of one finger.
"Hurry up, or you'll be late for school."

The weird thing is,
as I pound down the driveway to catch the bus,
I'm not thinking about Mom.
I'm remembering Blue.
The birdhouses are great...exactly what I wanted.

Dad's in the workshop

when I get home from school,
scraping yellow birch.
"Dad, do you know why
Mom covered up my table?"
He shakes his head.
"Will you ask her?"
"No."

Right, Dad. Let's not rock
the friggin' dory.

Twig and me march nonstop

to the falls
at the bottom of Seven Days Work.
I'm outta breath,
I'll be late for supper,
and I'm still pissed.

Twig gulps half the brook.

The falls are a long tumble of water that catches on granite
and spurts sheets of bubbles—
                    the sound of
                                        fits
                    and starts.

I toss Twig a Milk-Bone.

"Let's climb to the top."
Although Seven Days Work
is more like a big hill
than a mountain,
it's not as easy as it looks.

Rocks
                    juniper
                              laurel
rocks
                    ferns
rocks.

Every time I slow down,
I see my table
hidden
like I made it out of rough-sawn lumber.

At the crest, where the brook
meets the edge
          and falls,
I straighten, panting,
and turn around.

Breath catches in my throat.

The sun's sinking over Labrador,
          the gulf waxed gold.
A cluster of little houses,
and then the barrens—
    long diagonal lines
        of rock and ravines
           gouged by glaciers—

you don't see the pattern when you're on the ground.

"We did it," I whisper to Twig.

Standing at the very edge, standing tall,
                 I holler my name
and listen as it's swallowed by the sky.

Big discussion

as I eat microwaved chicken and soggy vegetables for supper—
yeah, I was late—
about Mom and Dad's wild weekend in St. John's.

Roxy and me want to stay home.
Mom wants us to stay with Uncle Mort and Aunt Gerd.

Roxy goes into logical-lawyer-mode,
ticking off each point on her fingers.

"You're only gone two nights.
Uncle Mort and Aunt Gerd live five minutes away.
We all have cell phones, so we can talk or text.
Nix is Mr. Good Behavior,
and the both of us know the rules—*right*, Dad?"

I nod a lot.

Mom says, "I suppose you can stay here....
We'll be trusting you to behave."

Dad says, pinning Roxy with his sternest look,
"Always take money for a cab, and no parties at the house."

He transfers *stern* to me. "Nix, look after your sister."

Mom tapes a list

of instructions, cautions, and emergency phone numbers
to the refrigerator.
She kisses me and Roxy good-bye
as if she's flying to Australia.
Roxy curls her lip.
I stand there like a dummy.
Dad urges Mom outside.
As he opens the truck door,
he says something and she laughs. Didn't take her long
                    to shuck off *parent*.

* * *

That night, Roxy has a date with Bryan.
"Where are you going?" I ask.
She twirls in a circle
like she's on a dance floor. "Out."
"Don't touch drugs or booze, you hear me?"

She flips her hair back, smiling dreamily.
"Bryan bought me these earrings,
I absolutely had to have them. He's so adorable."

Adorable like the shark in *Jaws*.

She fingers the earrings—delicate copper coils.
"I'm in love with him.
                    Utterly
                        and divinely
                    in love."

Oh, man. Roxy never goes gooey on me.
She dates a guy, wraps him around her skin-tight sweater,
and drops him, next victim already singled out.
   Team Deathmatch
      ten points per kill.
"Rox, be careful. Word is,
he dumps his girlfriends after a month."
"He's never dated me before. Besides, it's already
five weeks."

I tried.

"Curfew's midnight."
"Yes, Mom."

I cross the yard to the workshop.
Bird's-eye maple.
Coping saw.
Nearly sixteen
and I've never
asked a girl
for a date.

Cutting the dovetails for Loren's box,
I forget about Roxy and the time
                  and even Loren.

It's 11:30 when I surface. I leave the carcass
on the bench and sweep the sawdust.
Ten minutes later, I've made popcorn,
I'm sitting back in Dad's recliner,
and I've surfed the channels
to Spike 628, guy stuff.

At 4 a.m. I wake up. Crick
in my neck. Cars
roaring round and round a racetrack.
Creepy feeling
that I'm alone in the house.
The fridge whirs.

No one in the upstairs bathroom.
No one in Roxy's bed.
Her entire wardrobe strewn over the room
like it was shot from a cannon.
No messages on my phone.
I text her.
No reply.

Call the cops?
911?

I clean my teeth.
My room is tidy.
Socks in the sock drawer
in rows
like nails in the nail cabinet
2d to 16d.

From my window,
I watch the waves—long black shadows
rushing toward the rocks.

Every ten seconds, the signals flash
on Bullet Reef and the Gizzard.

It's 9:06 Saturday.

No messages from the RCMP
or St. Jerrold Hospital.

Mom calls at ten.
"Yeah," I say, "everything's fine.
Roxy's still asleep...
quit worrying, Mom,
we're fine. Just fine."

I wander around the living room
                    like Roxy's gonna pop up
from behind the chesterfield.
All you can see of my table
is the bottom of the two front legs.
I should toss Mom's vase through the window,
stuff the cloth in the garbage,
and lug the table into the front hall.

I should put six wet glasses on it.

I watch junk TV.

Bryan drops Roxy off at noon.
I grab her arm. "Where the *hell* have you been?"
"Let go—I have to shower and do my hair.
          Big party at Lara's tonight."
"We're having dinner with Aunt Gerd tonight."
"No, Nix, *you're* having dinner with Aunt Gerd."
"And what'll I tell her?"
"Tell her I've gone to St. Jerrold.

Tell her I've gone to Manhattan.
I don't care what you tell her!"
"I've already covered your ass once today—
why didn't you text me that you'd be out all night?"

As if she's picking up
a dead rat, Roxy lifts my hand
off her arm. "So bring up the fight
about the Iron Maiden t-shirt I borrowed."
"You didn't borrow it, you—"
"You're such a dipstick."

* * *

I pack some sandwiches.
Twig and me hike to the base of Seven Days Work.
She wallows in the brook,
shakes herself head to tail,
shakes a spray of rainbows.
Then she curls up at my feet and falls asleep.
I eat my sandwiches.
The blackflies eat me.

The brook burbles and slurps
over the rocks.
        If nobody's here
to hear it, it doesn't make a sound.

On the way home,

I see Blue scrambling up a ravine,
binocs swinging from her neck.
She waves at me and points to the sky.
"The ospreys are back!"

     I peer upward.
                Those two little specks?

But her face—she looks so darn happy.
I remember the first time I made a dovetail
that fit—really fit—
              Twig wuffs and runs toward her.
My voice rough, I say, "What's the big deal
with a couple of birds?"

She looks me in the eye.
"Those two birds could've flown
all the way from South America—
from as far south as Argentina.
Think about it. Just think about it."

"It's like wood that I've sanded and polished—
when the sun falls on it, it's—hell, I dunno."

"*We'll* never be the most popular kids in high school,"
Blue says, and suddenly we're both laughing.

She adds, "Nix, I'm really glad you're walking Twig.
I bet Swiff Dunphy never lets her off the chain."

If I don't get outta here, I'll be telling her
I love the stupid dog.
"Gotta go."

I walk away. Weirdest conversation
I ever had. But it kept my mind off

my sister and Bryan Sykes.

Roxy comes home

Sunday morning.
She looks
    overfed and ravenous
    cranky and smug
    hyper and exhausted.
She sleeps
all afternoon.

                * * *

Mom left a beef noodle casserole
in the freezer. I heat it in the oven
and lay the table. Mom and Dad
get out of the truck.

Dad puts the suitcase down,
pulls Mom close, and they kiss.
Like, for real.
I don't want to watch
and I can't stop watching.
I duck
so they won't see
I've been spying on them
and work on getting my face
in order.

By the time they make it to the kitchen,
I've got the oven door open and
I'm sticking a fork in the noodles.
They're cold in the middle.

The hot weather

vanishes overnight. Ice pellets
are bouncing off the dirt road,
crunching underfoot.

I don't bother with a leash
now that I'm Twig's pack.
She trails behind me to the kennel
with its moat of frozen mud,
droops as I fasten
the chain to her collar.

After I cross the grass—spears of ice—
and jump the ditch,
three sharp barks
cut through the hiss of sleet.
My head whips around.
Twig lifts her muzzle
            and howls
                    a long drawn-out howl
        wild and lonely, a howl
of despair.

Ice melting on my cheeks,
I stumble down the hill.

Mom's cooked roast chicken again,

with stuffing, cranberries, and gravy.
Might as well be cardboard.
As she doles out cottage pudding, I blurt,
"Mom, I want to buy Swiff Dunphy's dog."

"Nonsense, Nixon. Would you like your tea now, Bertram?"

"She's the dog I've been walking. Her name's—"
"Absolutely not," Mom says.

"She's well-behaved," I say, "you'd like her.
And I'd take care of her."

Mom puts a bowl full of cake and hard sauce
in front of me. "Eat up, there's lots more."
"She wouldn't be any trouble, really
she wouldn't—and I'd pay the vet bills."

Finally it sinks in that I mean business.

Mom says, "Dog hair? Fleas?
Muddy feet tracking my clean floors?
No, Nixon, we're not having a dog.
I don't want to hear another word about it."

"Dad?" I say. "I could build a kennel outdoors,
she could live there. Fix up a line across the backyard
                              so she could run.
I named her Twig. She's a real nice dog—
Swiff keeps her chained up all the time."
"You heard your mother, Nix."

"Twig's lonely. She needs me!"

Dad blows on his tea.

Roxy says with a smirk, "Bryan and me
drove up that way on Sunday.
Scrawniest excuse for a dog he ever saw—
crawling with tapeworms, he figures."

Before I know it, I'm halfways
across the table. "That's *his* crap—
don't you have any opinions of your own anymore?"

She looks startled. Almost scared.

"Sit down, Nix!" Dad thunders.
I shove back my chair, which tips
backward, bounces on the floor. The noise
scrapes my brain.
Muscles tight, I set the chair upright,
walk out of the room,

and take the stairs,
feet like mallets. Dead silence
from the kitchen.

I stand by my bedroom window.

Clouds low over the gulf.
The boughs of the silver birch
weighed down with ice.

Mom acts like nothing's

happened. Dad makes me
apologize to Roxy:
definition of *hypocrisy.*
As we wait for the bus, Roxy says,
"Fifteen-year-old guys don't go around
rescuing strays
that look like the arse-end
of a hyena. They hit on girls—
haven't I taught you anything?"
Two-word reply involving *f.*

That afternoon, Roxy gets off the school bus

ahead of me and walks up the driveway, shoulders
    slumped.
"What's wrong?" I say, even though I'm not talking to her.
"Nothing!"
I catch up with her. "C'mon, Rox, you can tell me."

Tears are glistening in her eyes.

She almost never cries
but when she does
it pulverizes me.

Did Bryan dump you?
The words won't come out.
"If Bryan was mean to you, I'll— "
"You'll what? Take out your MP5?"

She yanks open the door and rips through the kitchen.
I kick off my sneaks in the porch. I hated it
when Linsey Stearnes used to cry in math class
after her mother died.

"What's wrong with your sister?" Mom asks
as if it's my fault.
"Dunno," I say.

    Bryan?
    Suzie?
    Lara?
    The entire grade twelve class?

Upstairs, I change into my old jeans,
the ones I use for walking Twig,
and wait.
Roxy comes out of the bathroom.

She looks smaller somehow.

      Shrunk.

She sees me, hesitates, then walks right into me
and rests her forehead on my chest.
"Hey," I say, "hey," and put my hands
on her shoulders. How can someone drive you
into the middle of next week and make you feel
like you'd slay sixteen dragons for her?

She pulls back.
My hands fall to my sides.

I say, and it's guesswork, "Don't let those snotty seniors
get under your skin."
      Her lashes flicker.
Would Roxy let a gaggle of girls get to her
      if Bryan wasn't being—

over her head
I catch sight
of a row of penciled numbers
down the doorframe.
Inspired, I say, "How about
you measure me?
It's been a while."

Her smile is nowheres near a yellow sun.
"Sure you trust your little sister?"

I tug the white plastic stool from under the sink
while she scrabbles in the drawer for the ruler.
Standing on the stool,
she balances the ruler on my head.
"Five feet eleven," she says. "You ever
                           going to stop growing?"
"I'm a whole inch taller than Dad."
"You'll have to take up basketball," she says,
flicking me on the cheek with her fingernail,
which she knows bugs the hell out of me.

Oh well. At least she quit crying.

I finish Loren's box.

The bird's-eye maple
shines softly in the light.

The inside lined with oiled black walnut.

Will Loren like it?

Will she think about me when she opens it?

Will she see that it was made with love?

* * *

Roxy dates Bryan on Friday,
hums her way up the stairs at midnight.
Copper earrings dangling from her lobes,
coiled like snakes.

* * *

Twig sits heavy as granite on my shoulders.
I curse Arnie Bellweather's letter,
delivered to our box
by mistake.

Dad's watching NHL

last period, Capitals vs Penguins. Mom's
gone to bed, tired from spring-cleaning their bathroom.
I'm chomping a molasses cookie.
    I owe Twig big time,
because now when I eat cookies, they don't
sink to a puddle around my waist.

In my pocket, my phone vibrates.
Bryan Sykes.
    roxy shitfaced

So I was right all along—
protective, caring and *respectful*—
fake as pressboard.

        Three years ago.
        Saturday afternoon,
    Mom and Dad in Corner Brook,
        Roxy and me home.
    I'm upstairs, she's downstairs.
        I'm craving
        Sprite with Tostitos.

Three empty Coke cans lined up on the kitchen table,
along with a half-empty bottle of Smirnoff Triple Distilled.
    Roxy lifts the bottle, misses her mouth,
        slops vodka on her t-shirt.
        Her smile off-center.
    "Lisa sold it to me," she says.

I screw the cap on the bottle.
She mewls a protest.

Even at twelve, I'm taller than her.
I wrap my arms around her middle
and hoist her up the stairs,
her feet fumbling for each step, legs buckling.
Pushing her into the bathroom, I say,
"Cold shower.
Then sleep it off.
If you write my French essay
I won't tell Mom and Dad."

I made 91 in French that week
and Roxy swore she'd never OD on booze again,
because hangovers were way beyond gross.

Until tonight, she's kept her word.

My thumbs get to work.
end of driveway when

10

Seconds? Minutes?

Game's in the last period,
Backstrom arguing with the ref.
"I think I'll work on the birdhouses, Dad.
I can sleep in tomorrow."
"Got your keys?"
"Yeah. Don't wait up—I'll let Roxy in."
"Quit your belly-aching."
Backstrom. Not me.

No Lexus in the driveway.
I unlock the workshop.

Sky nailed with stars.

Bryan's Lexus pulls up

nine minutes later. I stride down the driveway, praying
Dad'll be riveted to the screen
by three goals in a row or a major fight.

Bryan climbs out. "She can't hold her liquor."
"She's underage!"
He lights up a cigarette, blows smoke
over the roof of the car. "That's her problem."
"If my father sees her drunk, it'll be your problem."
"You threatening me?"

Blood's in a torrent through my veins.
He's taller than me, although I've got more
heft. I'd like to slam my fist into the sneer on his face.
Can't start a fight with Dad still up.
Start a *fight?*

"If I ever threaten you," I say, "you'll know it."
"Get her out of my car!"
"Who do you think you are, Tony Soprano?"
Bryan steps around the hood. "The evening I met you,
I didn't like the look on your face,
and I don't like it now."
Glaring back, I open the passenger door. "C'mon, Roxy,
we gotta hurry—Dad's still up."

She's slumped against the dashboard.
No seat belt.
Screw Bryan Sykes.
And where are the cops when you need 'em?

I haul her arm over my shoulder
and ease her out of the car,
staggering under her weight.
She mumbles, "Leave me 'lone."
As I kick the door shut,
Bryan says, "You're a good boy, Nixon."

He climbs into the Lexus and guns the engine.
His jazzy red tail lights
disappear around the corner.

Roxy's ankles

aren't doing their job.
"Stand up, Rox! We're going to the workshop.
If Dad sees you like this, you'll be grounded
until you're a grandmother."

We veer up the driveway. Using my hip,
I lever her over the threshold.
She throws her arms around my neck,
        her kiss grazing my cowlick
because I duck. I shove her backward onto the couch.
"You so blitzed you don't know
who you're kissing?"

"It was a girls' thing...who could drink the most
of those pretty pink coolers.... I showed 'em...
                smart-ass seniors."
You gotta admire Roxy. Not one slurred s.

Her face turns the color
of iceberg lettuce. Her head thunks
to her knees. "Gonna puke."

Omigod. I hustle her to the bathroom
in the back corner of the workshop,
shut her in,
and listen to her heave.

Eventually, she flushes the toilet.

I open the door,
turn on the cold tap full blast,

and thrust my unsuspecting sister
under it.
Head only.
She shrieks, arms
thrashing. I grip her scalp,
Vampire Red hair streaming between my fingers.

When I'm good and ready,
                    I let go.
She whirls,
spray, cusswords, and fists
flying.
Her ring catches my cheekbone.
In the mirror over the sink,
we watch
two drops of blood
ooze to the surface.
Mom won't believe a chisel did that.

I say hoarsely, "You're so frickin' clueless—
I'm trying to save your skin!"

She leans against the wall,
closing her eyes.
Water trickles down her face.

* * *

At my workbench,
I stare at the drainage holes
in the birdhouse.
I pick up a screwdriver,
then put it down.
My hands are trembling.

I drill enough screws

in the birdhouses
that Dad won't get suspicious.
Half an hour's gone by.
Roxy hasn't spoken
one word to me.

She pushes herself up from the couch.
Her hair's still wet.
She wavers past me
(the cops would flunk her),
tugs the door open,
and totters outside.
I unplug the drill and follow her.

Dad's gone to bed.
She makes it up the stairs
without tripping.
Goes into her room.
Locks the door.

First thing Sunday, Mom says,

"Nixon, whatever happened to your face?"
"Cut it. Shaving."
"It looks as though someone scratched you."
"Old blade, Mom."

* * *

Roxy doesn't get up
until Mom and Dad have gone for a drive.
Then she spends two hours in the bathroom.
I'm right there
when she comes out. Sarcasm
thick as sour milk, I say, "Thanks a lot
for sobering me up last night."

She flicks her hair. She's glued strands
of green glitter to her scalp. "I've learned my lesson
about those pretty pink coolers—
and I could've gotten past Dad."
"Garbage truck cart away your brains?"
"Bryan would've looked after me."
"Bryan couldn't wait to be rid of you."
"That's because you were interfering!"
"Just because *his* initials are BS,
you don't have to be full of it!"
Bleep her reply.

Tuesday night, as Dad and me leave

Tim Hortons, Bryan Sykes is outside, five girls
clustered around him and his Lexus.
        He's putting the moves
on a chick with blond streaks and a giggle
that files my teeth.
His hand on the back of her neck,
his lips sliding down her cheek.
Dad's too busy rolling up the rim to notice.

I'm still mad at Roxy
and I always thought I was an advocate of non-violence,
but for the second time
I'm ready to plough Bryan Sykes on the kisser.
I better take boxing lessons.
Starting now.

Back home, we stow the boards Dad bought
on the rack in the workshop,
then I go upstairs and rap on Roxy's door.

She yanks it open. "What do you want?"
"You dating Bryan this weekend?"
Her eyes flick to her phone. "I just texted him.
He'll get back to me."

"When I was in town with Dad, I saw him outside Tims.
Him and all these—"
"He's a popular guy."
"Roxy, he was—"
"The most popular guy in the school."

The look she gives me shrivels my—
return to checkpoint, change weapons.

I stick my thumbs in my pockets. "You know what?
Chasing Bryan Sykes ain't the way to go.
                              Play hard to get."
"Since when did you hang out your shingle?"
"Bryan's like the rest of us guys.
Hunters from way back. Just ask the woolly mammoth."

"You? Out hunting *girls?*"
"You've lasted nearly two months," I say. "That's a long time
for Bryan."
"He won't dump me," Roxy says
confidently. "I'm different."

Maybe I don't talk much
because it's a waste of air.

I'm in the cafeteria eating the Thursday special,

which the cook calls "Mac Cheese"
but I call yellow cement,
when Loren sits down across from me.

A noodle goes down my windpipe.
I choke. My eyes water. My cheeks broil.

She says, with that quiet smile of hers,
"The box is beautiful, Nix—thank you."

Loren Cody is sitting with me in the cafeteria.
I want this moment to last forever.
                              For all eternity.
"Um...you're welcome," I say.
Oh, God, why am I such a dork?

"Chase told me about your workshop. Could you make
a picture frame for my mom's birthday in June?"

I nod. Several times.

"Fabulous," she says. "I'll come over with Chase
some evening and bring the photo
so you can measure the size of the frame."

The bell shrills.
I nearly jump out of my seat. She gets up, smiles again,
and walks away.
I dump the macaroni in the trash.

* * *

I'm in French class when it hits me. Her eyes
aren't nearly as blue as Blue's. *Bleu...plus bleu...*

"*M'sieur* Humbolt!
The past perfect of the irregular verb *aller*."

As we're walking up the driveway,

Roxy starts in on me. "You made a total ass yourself
in the cafeteria today. Glomming onto
Loren Cody like she's—"
"Of course, you never glom onto Bryan Sykes."
"Bryan and I are an item!"
"I wouldn't be too sure of that."
"I don't believe this—my own brother
wants the guy I love to ditch me."
"No, I don't," I say, which is likely a lie,
but the way her voice wavered...
                        We've reached the door.
I stub my toe on the step.
No point repeating what I say.

Serious distance

between me and my sister,
that's what I need.
So Twig and me start out
on our regular afternoon walk, and if I'm
traveling at top speed, Twig's not complaining.

A girl's standing by the side of the road past Swiff's.
Twig wriggles with pleasure and tugs at the leash.
I march toward her.
I'm not in the mood for Blue McCallum.
I'm not in the mood for anyone.

Or am I just scared I'll run off at the mouth again
because there's something about her...but the girl
who's patting Twig isn't...
        I say foolishly, "You've cut your hair."
"Mom talked me into it."

Dark gleam, like feathers. Her smooth skin,
        her cheekbones, her soft mouth,
                which I never noticed before.
"It looks nice."

"Thanks." She adds, awkward for her,
"I've been waiting for you—I need to talk to you."

She's not smiling. Jeez. What's up?
"Let's cross the highway so I can let Twig off the leash."

The ponds are the color of old pennies. Snow
still draped over The Three Brides.
Twig puts her nose to the ground, whuffing up smells
like she's a vacuum cleaner.

Blue turns to face me. "It's about Roxy."

Face, voice, throat—they all go tight. "Yeah? What about her?"
"Are you going to listen?"
"Roxy's rock bottom on my list right now."

Blue's lips are jammed together.
Her hair electric in the sun.
She takes a deep breath. "When I was in the washroom
this afternoon, I overheard Suzie talking to Lara—
I guess Roxy got drunk at a party on Saturday, and humiliated Bryan
in front of his friends. Today he told Suzie,
who's the worst gossip in the school,
that he's planning on dumping Roxy."

My turn to take a deep breath. "He dumps everyone
        sooner or later."
"But he won't have the decency
to tell Roxy himself—you know that, and so do I."
"Suzie could be making it up."
"I don't think so...you see, he's already got his eye
on someone else. Kristen, the girl in grade twelve
with the blond streaks."
"I know. I saw him with her."
"You have to warn Roxy."
"I did! She wouldn't listen."
"Then try harder."
"You ever tried to warn Roxy
about anything? Good luck is all I can say."
"Nix, she's your sister!"
"Tell me something I don't know!"
"Shoot the messenger, why don't you?"

Right. Where's my MP5.

I try to wriggle the tension from my shoulders.
I've had a bellyful of Roxy, Blue, Suzie, Lara,
                        and girls in general.
"I appreciate you telling me all this, Blue—"
"No, you don't."
"Okay, so I don't."
"I'll talk to her tomorrow," Blue says, "when we get off the bus."
"Stay out of it!"

Twig whines.

Her voice ice clear through, Blue says, "I sure will."
She pivots and heads for the ravine.

It takes me five minutes to cool down.
Another five to realize
I'm gonna have to grovel. Big time.

It's only a haircut.

* * *

By the time I get home, Dad's driven Roxy
to Kaitlin's, for supper and to study for a history test.
I tape a message to her door.
I NEED TO TALK TO YOU!!

When she comes upstairs at 9:30, I'm on the phone
with Chase. He finishes his story about the coach
whose nose was broken—bloodily—by a puck.
I push End

just as Roxy slides the same piece of paper under my door.
SUCK IT UP
The letters make deep grooves in the paper.

I bang on her door, try the handle.
Locked.
Is this when Blue would call in the Marines?

Roxy checks her phone

as we're finishing supper on Friday. She gasps,
gripping the phone like it's a stun gun.

Mom says placidly, "Help me load the dishwasher, Roxanne."
"I'm going upstairs."
Dad says, "Do what your mother asks."

She erupts. Jabbing the phone at him,
she cries, "If you weren't so damn cheap,
you'd buy me a car. Then I'd have a social life
instead of being stuck in this godforsaken backwater!"

"Three months after you got your novice licence," Dad says,
"you put a dent in the truck."

"No date?" I say, trying to keep any hint
of *I told you so* out of my voice.
Her eyes—brilliant with rage and, yep, pain—
skewer me to the wall.
"If you weren't such a wimp,
guys would pay more attention to me."
"Don't blame me because Bryan Sykes is a scumbag!"

She scrapes her chair back,
runs upstairs, and slams her bedroom door so hard
I swear the walls shake.

She plays wall-shaking music
all evening,

and doesn't appear until noon the next day,

eyes
red,
fingernails
black.

My new gig is jogging

(well, shuffling) to Swiff's,
this being more like
Twig's regular pace
than walking
and not as awful
as I thought it would be.
Steady westerly
keeps the blackflies away.

Usually Twig hears me
panting my way uphill
before she sees me.
I put on a burst of speed
to impress her.

     Except

she isn't there.
I stop.
She's gotta be.

Gulping in air, I wipe sweat
from my eyes.
Chain's gone,
metal post pulled out of the mud.
Bowl's gone. No smoke
from the chimney, no truck
parked in the driveway. No
neighbors who'd know
where Swiff is, where Twig is.

Nothing
but a ramshackle old house,
dead grass with a few spikes of green,
and an empty kennel.

My heartbeat thrums in my ears.
Do something, Nix.

Like what?
Run around the barrens looking for her
when it's obvious
Swiff's taken her away?

I sit on the front steps and wait.
Wait
for one hour, two, three...

I never thought I had much
imagination until today.

She's been howling at night,
so he's driven her up Sugar Loaf
and put a bullet
through her skull.

or

He's put her in a sack and
thrown her
off the wharf.

or

Last night
he took her
to the pound
in St. Jerrold...

which is closed
on weekends and
which is where they
kill the dogs
no one wants.

Who'd want Twig?
I love that fricking dog,
but even I
have to admit
she's no beauty.

At five after six,
I get up from the step
and start down the hill.
I feel ninety years old.
Mom better not ask
why I'm late
for supper.

Swiff's old truck

yaws through the potholes.
I'm on the front porch.
Sunday afternoon. Fog
    so thick
we're cut off from the rest of the world.

Swiff climbs out of the truck,
         his face a mix
of defiance and cunning. "Hey, kid."
I stand up. "Where's Twig?"
"Twig? What kinda fool name is that?"
"Where's the dog?"
"Well now," he says, taking the last cigarette
from a battered pack,
then tossing the pack on the grass.
He flicks the lighter,
draws in a good breath of cancer.
"Now you gotta understand I'm an ol' guy
with not much in the way of hard cash
and that dog— "
"Where *is* she?"
"Sold her," he says.

It's like hitting your thumb with a hammer.
Takes a minute for the pain to reach you.
"Sold her? Who to?"
"That ain't your business."

I take the steps slowly.
"Who to, Swiff?"

He looks scared.
        Power
surges through my veins,
heady as that rum Roxy stole
out of Uncle Mort's cupboard
on my eleventh birthday.
I seize a handful of his denim jacket.
"You're gonna tell me
if we have to stand here until tomorrow."
"Okay, okay...dunno why
you're makin' such an all-fired fuss
over a dog that's sculpin-ugly. Arnie offered me—"
"Arnie Bellweather? The fellow
whose letter came to our place?"
"Right on," he says sullenly.
"I remember, he lives in Sharkey Bay."
"Now listen to me—don't you go messin'
with Arnie. He'll have your guts on a plate."
"You didn't even have the guts to tell me!"

I let go of his jacket,
scrub my palms down my damp jeans,
and walk off into the fog.

I go to school, like normal,

slip away from the crowd of kids streaming in the main door,
run to the bank machine,
then to the drug store
to wait for the municipal bus that goes south
every weekday morning.

> I'm nearly sixteen.
> Time I found out what
> *Absent without excuse*
> feels like.

The bus follows the highway
for an hour or more, ducking
into the communities that line the coast,
the gulf steel-gray,
the mountains pushing farther and farther inland.

> All I have is a name—
> Arnie Bellweather—
> a snarl
> alongside a sunny day in summer.

Finally we turn into Sharkey Bay,
where houses, a gas station, and a church
sprawl along a cobble-stone beach.
The bus pulls up outside the convenience store.
I get off.
Wonder what to do next.
Slouch
into the store and ask for Arnie.

The woman behind the cash
—red slash of lipstick—
says, "Take the highway south, first turn east,
couple empty houses on your left.
Arnie's is the last house on the road."

She leans over the counter.
"His mood shifted from middling-bad
          to poison
when his wife upped and left three weeks ago
along with the two kids,
and it'd be a hard go to find one soul in Sharkey Bay
          who blames her.
You got business with him?"

"Thanks for your help," I say,
and I'm outta there.

The road east is a dirt road across the barrens, no place to hide
except a single clump of spruce
with a scramble of
alders, dogwood, and choke-cherry.
Two rundown bungalows with lop-sided
          For Sale signs,

then Arnie's place.

Arnie's house

sits squat as a toad
in a mess of mud, lumber, torn Tyvek, busted shingles,
and pink puffs of fibreglass.

    In the open
where the sun will beat down on it,
is a plywood kennel.
Metal post, straggle of chain,

    Twig
lying with her chin on her paws,
so still she could be dead.

"Twig!" I shout.
Her head jerks up.
She leaps to her feet and dashes to the limit of the chain,
       which flings her back
and the whole time she's barking,
barks so joyous that everything

blurs.
I run toward her.

A man bursts out the front door. "Git away from my dog!"

I'm on my knees in the mud,
Twig slurping kisses
all over my face,
her tail like a wiper blade at full speed

      when a boot comes from nowhere.

She yelps, thrown sideways.
I'm on my feet. "Hey!"

Arnie Bellweather is big. Bigger than big.
He shoves his face at mine.
"You tellin' me what to do?"
"N-nossir."
"Good—now git."

Twig's gone quiet.

Coarse black hairs grow out of Arnie's nose and ears,
his brows crawling over his glass frames
      like spiders.
Behind his head, a crow circles lazily.

I can't just run away.
     I can't.
"I-I need to talk to you,"
I say. "I want to buy your dog.
I used to walk her for Swiff Dunphy—
I'll pay you twice what you paid him."

"Dumb as ditchwater you are—I got no use
     for your money."

My hand's unsteady as I tug my wallet
out of my pocket. How did Twig get to be
so goddamned important?
I fumble for some bills. "Cash."

"She's a limp excuse for a guard dog, but I'm keepin' her."
"With the money, you can buy a better dog."

     Picking me up by the elbows like I'm nothing
but a gull feather, he lifts me off the ground until

my face is level
with his.
"I'm only gonna say this once.
Git off my property
and don't come back."

He drops me. I stagger. My elbows feel
as if they've been through a gravel crusher.

Twig cowers at the end of her chain,
ears back,
body low.
So this isn't the first time he's kicked her.

I walk away.

Coward
coward
coward...

This isn't Modern Warfare,

I'm not in the U.S. Marines,
and Arnie's place isn't Creek or The Bog.
But somehow I gotta respawn.
Tail between my legs
like Twig's after he kicked her.

He kicked my dog.

I let that thought simmer.
At the clump of trees, I cross the ditch
and tuck myself under some skinny boughs,
out of sight of the road.
Shuck off my backpack, take out my sandwiches,
made by Mom.
Mosquitoes whine.
Slug of water to wash down tuna and lettuce on white bread.
Save the cookies for later.
Tug my ball cap low as it'll go and spray on fly dope.
Be prepared, that's me.
Prize idiot—thought I'd just have to
wave a few bills under Arnie Bellweather's
(disgustingly hairy) nose
and Twig would be mine.

The bus goes north at 4:30.
That gives me four hours to spring my dog.
I text Roxy to cover for me after school.
    Then I wait.
You'd think by now I'd be better at it.

Arnie belts past

in his black Dodge half-ton
exactly two hours later. I race
up the road and unclip Twig's chain.
We run back to the trees, burrow
into the shrubs, Twig
pressed against me, my pulse flapping
like a stranded mackerel.

Now what?
Can't risk Arnie seeing me.
Can't stay here.
Can't miss the bus.
I never thought this through.
 Good at dovetails.
 A right shag-up
 when it comes to real life.

If Arnie's just going for the mail,
he could be back anytime.
Or he could be gone for hours.
I chew my lip.
Best plan is to head north along the highway
and hitch a ride. If I see Arnie's truck,
I'll hide Twig in the ditch.

Leaving the shelter of the trees
is downright terrifying.
Ears on high alert,
I say, "C'mon, Twig,"
and as we hurry down the road we practice

Go! Lie down!
until she rushes into the ditch,
splashing water every which way.

She thinks it's a game.

We reach the end

of the dirt road. Not one speck of cover.
I turn right onto the highway so we're aiming
north. Five minutes
will bring us to the Sharkey Bay turnoff.
"Let's go," I say, and start jogging,
Twig bounding beside me, tongue
lolling.

An eighteen-wheeler roars past, back-draft
cuffing me sideways.
My lungs hurt.
My muscles hurt.
I'm
slowing
down.
Twig sniffs a bush and pees.

A black half-ton's
parked outside the gas station
in Sharkey Bay.
I take to my heels like
the devil's on my tail.

When I hear cars coming behind me,
I turn, stick out
my thumb.
Whoosh
of air and
they're gone.

If Arnie leaves now, Twig
and me are toast.

Vehicle with a broken muffler.
I twist,
thumb out.
Green pick-up, more rust than truck,
old lady at the wheel.
She stops on the shoulder. Over my shoulder,
I glimpse big Arnie Bellweather stumping
out of the gas station.
                    I haul the door open.
She has flyaway
white hair, grimy hands.
She looks at me and frowns.
"I seen you before."
                    I shake my head.
"Then who d'you put me in mind me of...? No
matter, it'll come to me. That there dog got fleas?"
"No, missus."
"Dog on the floor. You gets the seat."

Arnie's driving toward the highway.
I bundle Twig in the truck,
scuttle in after her.
Can't work the seat belt
because my hands are shaky.
The old lady checks her rearview mirror.
I sneak a glance through the back window.
The black truck is going south.

South is good.

"Runnin' away from home?"

the old lady asks.
"No!"
"At odds with the cops?"
"No."
Not yet, anyways.
Twig rests her head on my knee.
I rub her between the ears.
The old lady says, "Where you headed?"
"Bullbirds Cove."
"You're deafenin' me with your chatter, b'y.
Gonna tell me your name?"
"Nix Humbolt."

She barrels along the highway, still frowning.
Seed packets scattered on the dash,
a bag of sheep manure on the seat between us.

She slaps her palm hard on the wheel.
"That's it! Neil Ardrich.
You're the spittin' image of Neil.
Same red hair. Same cowlick."
She gives me a triumphant look.

"Never heard of him."
        Spitting image?
Only spitter in my life
is Swiff Dunphy.

She says, "Not him nor his wife?
Now what was her name—Elaine?"

"No."
"Tragic, what happened," she says. "The both of them
died in a motel fire
in Corner Brook. That'd be..."
            another frown, "thirty-three year ago
April-month.
Left a little tyke, about seven. Pretty little thing.
Went into a foster home, that's what I heard.
Sad."

I gape at her. Add seven and thirty-three
and what do you get?

Mom just turned forty.

"What was her name?" I whisper. "The little girl."

"Laurel? Cora? Coral! Seems the older
I gets, the more I remembers
from back then—but don't you go askin' me
what I ate for breakfast."

Coral. Mom's name.

Twig's fur
        rough under my fingers.

We pass Betty's Head, Horseshoe Harbour,
and Finback Cove, where
twenty of their thirty-six men
drowned one August morning
in a sudden squall.

            Me aged six or so, asking Mom why Kendel Green
            had four grandparents and I only had two.

"They're dead," she said
and pushed me out to play.

The old lady lost in her thoughts. My thoughts—
they won't quit their scurrying long enough
to be called thoughts. As we reach Bullbirds Cove,
the old lady says, "You ask your mom and dad
'bout Neil Ardrich."

"I will. Thanks for picking us up."

She shakes her head. "Spittin' image," she says,
and drives away.

At Godsell's Convenience Store

I buy a box of dog food, then Twig and me
go out on the barrens so I won't arrive home
before the school bus.

She scarfs the food, drinks
from a bog-hole, and sticks
close. I try to forget
Neil Ardrich and his wife Elaine
long enough to plan my strategy.

Maybe I won't need a strategy.

At twenty after four, I run up the driveway
with Twig bouncing beside me.
Dad steps out of the workshop.

"Hi," I say.
"That the dog you been walking?"
I nod.
"Your mom just scrubbed the floor. Keep it outside."
"Dad, I bought the dog. She's mine."
"You had no business doing that, Nix.
Your mother doesn't want a dog."

Right on cue, Mom comes outside, along with Roxy.

"Mom, this is Twig. I own her now—
I bought her. I'll rig up a line outdoors
and exercise her every day. She'll be no trouble."

Mom's frowning. "You *bought* her? From Swiff Dunphy?"

"Well...yeah."
"I'm sure he'll give you your money back."
"Mom, *please*...she howls when I put her on the chain,
and I can't stand it."
"So she'll howl all day when you're in school
and she's chained in our yard."
"No, she won't. She'll be happier here."
"Take the dog back, Nixon."
"I can't! I mean—Swiff's gone away
for a couple days. She could stay in the workshop
until I build a kennel."

That's when Swiff Dunphy's truck pulls into our driveway.
Swiff yells, "Kid, you stole Arnie's dog!"
Mom says, "There's no need to shout, Mr. Dunphy."
"Damn right there is! Your kid stole that dog.
In broad daylight. From Arnie Bellweather in Sharkey Bay.
I tol' Arnie I'd get his dog back,
and that's what I'm here to do."

Dad's voice is as quiet as Swiff's was loud.
"Is this true, Nix?"
"I offered Arnie twice what he paid. It wasn't really stealing."
His eyes sandpaper my face.
"Did you steal the dog?"
"He kicked her! I couldn't leave her there."

Dad walks toward me.
He takes the leash from my hand.
He tugs Twig across the driveway.
He passes the leash to Swiff.
"I'm sorry for the trouble Nix has caused,"
he says. "He'll pay for your gas
and he'll write Mr. Bellweather an apology."

Swiff grins at me, cocky
as a bull terrier.
"Too bad, kid."

"Mom, Dad," I say hoarsely, "you can't do this!
Arnie's mistreating her."

"Yeah," Roxy says, "I'm with Nix.
The dog could stay outdoors—get a life, guys."

Eyes like flint, Dad says, "That's enough!
If a dog's being mistreated,
you go through the proper channels.
You don't steal someone's property, then lie to your parents."

Swiff drags Twig nearer the truck.
She's looking over her shoulder,
a pitiful look...*rescue me.*

At least Mom isn't immune.
She says, "Bertram, don't you think we—"
"The dog goes back where it belongs."

Swiff dumps Twig in the back of the truck,
fastening the leash to a rusty lawnmower
that's wedged against some birch logs.
"Don't you come near my place again, kid,"
he says and reverses down the driveway, the truck
snarling louder than Arnie.

I *won't* cry.
Not in front of Dad.

He says, "Go to your room, Nix. Your allowance is cut off
and you'll stay away from the workshop
for the next two weeks."

I push past Mom and Roxy.
Cutting off my allowance.
Making me write a jeezly letter.

Dad. Swiff. Arnie.
Bastards, all of 'em.

Ten minutes later, my sister

walks into my room. I'm sitting on the bed, head
in my hands. "Get lost, Rox."

She says, talking fast, "I'm sorry for what happened
with Swiff, and for being so mean about the dog last week."

I look up. "No kidding?"
"Do I look like I'm kidding?"
"Guess not...what made you change your mind?"

Her grin flashes, the grin I haven't seen much of
lately. "You cut school."
"I only made things worse."
"You broke the rules. *You.* That's major, bro—
you must love that ugly mutt."
"Watch it. I kinda like the way she looks."
She grins again. "Love's blind, right?"
I tug at my cowlick. "Yeah, I love Twig...of course I do.
Why else do you think I've hung in this long?"

"Good on ya." Then her eyes
narrow. "I just had a big bust-up
with Mom and Dad. In the driveway,
for all the neighbors to hear.

Listed every reason I could think of
why we need a guard dog,
from Dad's Fine Furniture
to Gram's silver teapot. Told 'em
the dog's dragged you out of the workshop
and made you lose ten pounds."
She scowls. "I should've saved my breath.
I don't know what's with Dad—does the guy
even *have* a heart?"

Ever since Swiff drove away,
it's like someone's had a choke-hold on my gullet.
Now Roxy being so helpful...so kind...

"Shit, Nix, you don't look too hot."

With a jolt, I realize it's happened again.
Roxy's back to Roxanne.
I never realize how much I miss Roxanne
until Roxy's nice to me.

I swipe at my eyes. "You ever hear of a man
called Neil Ardrich? Or his wife Elaine?
From Sharkey Bay?"

Puzzled, she shakes her head.
I describe the old lady and the little girl who was orphaned
thirty-three years ago at the age of seven.
"Spitting image, that's what she kept saying."

"You think they could be our other grandparents?"

"It would explain why Mom's so touchy about relatives."

Roxy asks questions, I fill in more details,
and we wonder out loud how we can prove anything

without asking Mom outright.
We haven't talked like this
since the summer I was five,
when I saw two dogs going at it
and Roxy told me about sex.
I didn't believe her—too bizarre.

Finally, we run out of words. She says awkwardly,
"I better crack my trig text—quiz tomorrow.
Thanks for telling me, Nix."

"Thanks for listening."

I stand up and give her
a bone-crunching hug.

I wake up the next morning possessed by a

rage
so total
so mega
that if I unleashed it
the way I unleash
Twig

everyone in my path
would have tapeworms
bursting out their ears
and die frothing
at the mouth
from rabies.

I'm in the lineup at the cafeteria,

trying to ignore Roxy, who's
hanging out
     at one of the seniors' tables,
hanging onto
Bryan's sleeve, laughing up at him,
adoration so blinding
it mortifies me to watch.

Suzie and her clique—
which includes Kristen, the chick with the blond streaks—
are watching, too.
Crows sighting carrion.
Suzie says something to Lara,
who laughs so loudly heads turn.
Including Bryan's.

He sees Blond Streaks.
Unlatching Roxy's hand,
he heads straight for her.

Roxy stands there like she's paralyzed.

Someone elbows me from behind.
"Move along, Humbolt."
I turn around, snarl at the guy,
and pick up my loaded tray.
Suzie's smiling at Roxy,
the kind of smile that slivers your spine.

Roxy hurries after Bryan, grabs his elbow,
and when he swings around, she starts pleading
with him, leaning into him
with her whole body,
desperation naked in her face.
  He shoots words at her.
She jerks backward.

I drop my tray.

Impressive
what a crash
one tray
makes on a tiled floor
and how far
Wednesday's special
—beef stew—
can splash.

Stew coats my sneaks
but who gives a damn?

Bryan's staring at me.
I give him the finger.

Chase high-fives me

on the school bus. "Neat diversion," he says.
Blue sits down beside me.
"You might want to move," I say, "my sneaks stink
of beef stew," and I don't sound over-friendly
even though five days ago on the barrens
I figured I'd have to do some major groveling
the next time I talked to Blue.

She says, "You took the pressure off Roxy."
"The day you and I met on the barrens, I tried
to warn her about Bryan. Didn't do one pick of good—
she told me to suck it up."
"At least you tried," Blue says fiercely.
Fierce.
"Is there anything you're afraid of, Blue?"

"Black bears. Black holes.
Black widow spiders,
and I've never even seen one."
She plucks at her jeans. "What if
I find a rabbit that's been hit by a car,
and it's so badly injured
I have to finish the job?"

I should've known I'd get the full-meal deal.

All week

I go through the motions
of school, meals, reviewing for exams.
Kids give me a wide berth
in the cafeteria lineup.

I freeze out Chase by the lockers.
Loren's smile comes from another planet.

The workshop's off-limits.

I don't toss Mom's vase
through the living room window
or her tablecloth into the garbage,
but it's a close call.

I don't talk to Dad.
Or Mom.
Or my sister,
who's in a foul mood
and hasn't even thanked me
for my beef-stew tactics.

I give up jogging.
I don't walk anywhere.

I don't think about Twig.

I can't stop thinking about Twig.

Friday afternoon,

Roxy clumps up the stairs
                 ahead of me.
Vampire Red has begun to fade, so last night
she dyed a neon-pink stripe over one ear.
As I go into my room, she pushes in after me.

"Get out!"
"When are you going to quit moping over the damn dog
                 and *do* something?"
I toss my books the bed. "Do *what*—
steal five thousand bucks from the credit union
and offer it to Arnie? Snatch Twig again,
hitchhike to St. John's, and become a panhandler?
Or should I hold Dad's old shotgun to his head
and tell him I'll blow his brains out
if he doesn't let me have the dog?"

"If I gave up on Bryan
as easy as you've given up on your dog,
he'd be dating someone else."
"He sure would. The chick with the blond streaks."
"Kristen? That skank?
                 Your problem is
you won't take control—go after what you want.
Seize the day and all that crap."
"I seized last friggin' Monday and it backfired."
"So try something else."
"Take your advice and shove it!"

She steps closer, poking me in the chest.

"Do what Dad says. Get—"
"Like I'm going to do anything he says."
"Get evidence. If Arnie's beating your dog,
video him doing it, then go to the cops.
The local corporal's an animal nut.
Adopted a cat with three legs. Found homes
for two puppies left in a dumpster.
      She'd be a soft touch."
Another poke. "Just get off your butt.
I can't stand watching you do zilch."

"A video," I say.
"Yeah...use your phone."
"The cops would impound Twig. As evidence."
Her fingernail drills into my t-shirt.
"See? Already you're talking yourself out of it."

A video...

Roxy notices the time

on my alarm clock.
"Gotta go! Pizza in town,
      then a party at Suzie's."
"Bryan picking you up?"
"Dad'll drive me." Her eyes flash. "But Bryan
will drive me home."

"I wish you'd give up on him."
"*Give up.* That your solution to everything?"
"He'll break your heart."
"I won't let him!"
"He's got his eye on Kristen. Hell, both eyes
      and both hands."
"I'm gonna fix her clock. Tonight."
I make myself say it. "Word is, Rox, he's ripe to dump you."

Roxy drags her fingers through her hair
      so it stands on end.
"I've never dated a guy yet who dumped me,
and I'm not starting with Bryan Sykes."
"What if you don't have a choice?"
"I can make Bryan toe the line.
Just watch me."
      Arms over her head,
she shimmies her hips like a belly dancer.
I may be her brother,
but I know *sexy* when I see it.
I know something else:
the world's overflowing with sexy girls.

Try spending fifteen minutes
in the corridors of St. Jerrold Consolidated—
sky-high testosterone, terminal swivel-neck.

Nails notching my palms, I say, "How can you love a guy
with a mean streak a mile wide?"
"Like you're the expert?"
"I've been in love with Loren for years."
            Which I did not mean to say.
Roxy says, "Ever had a date with her?
Ever had a date with anyone? Life's meant to be lived,
                not watched from the sidelines."
"How many times do I have to tell you
I don't live inside a freaking box?"
She says, real smug, "Got you that time, didn't I?"
"So chasing after Bryan is your idea of life?"
"You bet," she says.
"Maybe Bryan's *your* box."

Her face hardens. "There's days you're *so* immature."
"If you for one minute think Bryan Sykes is in love with you,
you're the one who's immature."
"Why do you think I've lasted longer than the rest?"
"Don't ask me."
"Because he *is* in love with me." She dissolves into one of her
sappy smiles. "He doesn't know how to handle it yet."
"Rox, don't go there."
"You're just envious of Bryan."
"*You're* dumber than dirt!"
She says bitterly, "I don't know why I bother
                trying to help you."
She tromps across the hall.
Her door slams.

I turf my French text to the floor.
Any idiot can see the only person Bryan Sykes loves
is Bryan Sykes.
But will Roxy listen to reason?
Not her. Not my stubborn, spitey sister.

I eat supper in silence, avoiding her eyes.
Back upstairs, I hear the shower
and the small sounds as she gets ready in her room.

But she did try to help me out.
If I had a video of Arnie kicking Twig...it's a decent idea.
Beats robbing the credit union.

I could knock on her door and thank her.
Instead, I press the power button on Xbox,
run down the list of who's online.
Like I care.

At seven sharp, she and Dad get in the truck and drive away.

Dad comes straight home.

It starts to rain.
Chase texts me: *L sick*
wanna catch movie

Who cares if I'm second choice?

Downstairs, Dad's watching the news channel.
"Can I go to the movies with Chase?"
"Have you written the letter to Arnie?"
I nod.
"Curfew's midnight," he says. "I want to read the letter
before you mail it."

In that case, Daddy-o, I better write it.

I climb in Chase's old Chevy.
Before I lose my nerve, I say,
"Sorry I didn't speak to you that day by the lockers."
"No prob."
But it is.

We leave Bullbirds Cove, tires
swishing on the wet highway.

"The dog I've been walking—Swiff sold her
to a guy in Sharkey Bay. So I stole her from him."
"You *what?*"
"Last Monday, and Dad made me give her back,
                and it made me so damn angry…"
Gathering speed as if I'm rolling downhill,
I tell him all about Swiff, Twig, and Arnie,

including his hairy nose,
and how I'm worried sick about my dog.

Chase listens. Really listens.

He says slowly, "Roxy's right, you need evidence—
a video's a great idea. Keep notes too.
Cops are hot on records."

I should've thanked her.

To my astonishment

it comes out almost natural. "How's Loren?"
Chase scrubs his scalp. "Girl stuff. Happens every month."

My cheeks turn redder than the scoreboard at the rink.

"Dad's banned me from the workshop," I say,
"so I can't make the frame for her mother."
"Her mom's birthday isn't until the end of June.
You can make it by then, can't you?"

Solved. So damn easy.
I feel the stirrings of hope
that somehow things will get better.
　　　I'll get Twig back.
　　　And Roxy'll figure out
that Bryan's a sleaze. She always was a smart rebel.
Told me once the first boy she kissed was a chain smoker—
"He tasted gross," she said, and crossed cigarettes
off her to-do list.

We watch *True Grit*.
For some reason, the girl called Mattie
reminds me of Blue.

Outside, the wind's shifted north,
squalls of rain slashing the parking lot.

We go for a pizza anyways, hoping
it'll let up. It doesn't. So we hit the highway,
Chase driving the same way he talks,
laidback but paying attention.

Pitch dark. Wipers on high.
We pass the police detachment
at the bottom of the hill.... I bet
the corporal would help out with Twig.

A couple minutes later we top the hill.
A cop car is parked near the ditch,
        red and blue light
        splashing the wet road.
Chase brakes. "Good thing our trunk's not full of beer."

Yellow tape strung along the ditch.
One cop is shining his flashlight over the rocks.
The other cop waves Chase on.
Both of them in yellow slickers,
their peaked hats covered in plastic,
        like shower caps.

"Likely someone hit a moose," I say.
Sometimes you see big—and I mean big—
smears of blood on the road.
One or two good rains and they're gone.

"They must've towed the vehicle away,"
Chase says. Then he tells me his plans
for hockey camp in July.

He lets me off in the driveway.
The surf sounds like bullets on the landwash.
I run for the house, rain streaming
        down my neck.
No truck.
How come Dad didn't say
they were going out? And why isn't he home
supervising my curfew?

In the mudroom, I shake out my jacket,
shuck off my wet sneaks.

"Mom?" I call. "Dad?"
No answer. "Roxy?"

The kitchen's empty. Coffee's in the pot,
a brick of cheese partly sliced on a plate,
a package of crackers
strewn
on the counter.

I rush

from room to room.
No one home but me.

Uncle Mort's angina acted up,
and Mom and Dad took him to the hospital—
that would explain the food left on the counter.
But you'd think they'd leave a note.

Roxy phoned and they've gone to pick her up.
Yeah, that's it—only reason
Dad would go out on a night like this.

But before he dropped her off, Dad would've checked
that she had money for a cab.

It must be Mom who's sick.

Dread sends me to the phone book,
where I grope through the pages,
searching for the hospital.
As I reach for the phone, I hear

the sound of tires
through the rain.
Headlights streak
the kitchen wall.
I close the phone book,
          knees weak.
Man, will I give them hell.

But it's not Dad who pushes into the mudroom.

It's Uncle Mort, his Blue Jays cap soaked through.
He takes off his glasses,
blinking at me. Face
like a bloodhound.
Dad got the looks in the family.

"Nixon—"
"What's going on? Where's Mom and Dad?"
"You have to come with me. Put on your jacket, it's raining."
"I know it's raining. Where are we going?"
"Hurry up," he says.

I thrust my arms into my slicker,
feet into my sneaks.
Check that I have my keys.
Shove him out the door.

As he backs down the driveway, I wonder
what I'll do if his angina does act up.
"Okay—where are we headed?"

"The hospital."
I blurt, "Is something wrong with Aunt Gerd?"
"No. I gotta concentrate on the road."

Of course there isn't anything wrong
with Aunt Gerd. Dad, not Uncle Mort,
would've come for me
if there was.
            Twig's dry
in her kennel and I doubt
Arnie'll bother her tonight.
I'll read the manual so I know how to work
the video on my phone.... Rain's
slackening off a little. Who *is* the man

with red hair who died in a motel fire?
                    Bilge
is what's swilling in my head,
because I can't land on anything and
I'm terrified to let my imagination loose
because of where it might lead me.

We turn into the hospital driveway.
Uncle Mort rolls down the window,
takes a ticket from the slot,
drops it on the dash.
        I just about scream at him
he's so damned slow.
He parks the car.

We duck our heads
and run to Emergency.
Empty cop car near the door.
I feel like I'm gonna upchuck.

Inside,

I wipe my sneaks on the black mat.
Uncle Mort tugs off his ball cap.
There's a nurse behind the desk,
her short-sleeved top covered
with loopy turquoise flowers.
She points down the corridor.

Rows of curtained cubicles,
a machine beeping.
Voices, someone
moaning. I smell
disinfectant.
Sickness.
Fear.

Uncle Mort taps on a door labeled Family Room
and pushes me inside.

Mom, her face blank,
like no one's home.
Dad, looking at me
as though he's never laid eyes on me before.
Aunt Gerd's snuffling, the tip of her nose red.
Dad gets to his feet, moving slow.

That's when it hits.
Mom. Dad. Me.
"Where's Roxy?"
        Mom makes a choked sound.
Aunt Gerd puts an arm around her.

Dad spaces his words as if he's
inventing them as he goes.
"There's been an accident."

"But...she's gonna be all right."
"No," he says.
"*No? What d'you mean?*"
                    His hands fall
on my shoulders.
Heavy.
I've never noticed all the lines
at the corners of his eyes.

"She's gone," he whispers.

Mom's still sitting there.
Staring at nothing.
Dad puts his arms around me,
holding on as though it's all he can do.

My slicker
drips
on the floor.

"Accident?" I say, my voice rising.
        "What kind of accident? In Bryan's Lexus?"
Dad shudders like I hit him with a whip.
"She was on the highway.
Walking home. In the middle of the road.
In the dark.
And the rain."

He drags in air. Keeps going.
"She was hit by a truck. The driver
stopped. Called 911. But

it was too late."

D.O.A.
One of her favorite bands.

My tongue feels thick. "I gotta see her."
"No," Dad says.
"Where is she? Mom, where is she?"
"You can't see her, Nix," Dad says.
"Why not? You're lying, aren't you? She's not
dead, she just—"
"Her face got banged up," he says. "Bad."

Mom makes another one of those sounds,
the kind Twig might make if someone was pulling out
her claws, one by one.

"Dad," I say, "I'm not a kid anymore.
She's my sister. I gotta see her."

He looks into my eyes.
My dad, stripped to the bare wood.

"Yes," he says.

An orderly leads Dad and me—
my feet dragging—
across the hall.

The room's small.

Single bed.
Side rails up.

Someone's lying there
under a clean white sheet. Crease marks
          sharp as knives.
Dad says, his voice breaking,
"It'll have to be a closed coffin."

The orderly draws back the sheet.

They've put a shower cap on her head.
Little purple daisies.
One side of her face scraped raw.
They didn't bother cleaning the dirt out.
Or the dried-up blood.

You're gonna remember this until the day you die.

Her mascara's smudged.
Like she was crying
before it happened.

Her eyes are closed.
I reach out a hand,
touch her cheek.
Cold.
Any minute, I'll wake up.

With the nails
of my right hand, I pinch the skin

on my left wrist.

Same room. Same creased sheet.

Leaning over, I kiss
her good cheek. Behind her ear,
a tuft of neon-pink hair on the pillow.
Why does she need a pillow?

I clear my throat.
"What happens next?"

"Funeral parlor," Dad says.

All alone? Lying on a slab in the dark?
Years ago, when we'd watch a horror movie, she'd miss
half of it because her eyes were tight shut.
My heart gives this big wallop in my chest.

       The orderly—
short guy in blue scrubs—
steps forward and picks up one corner of the sheet.

I grab him by the elbow. He drops
the sheet, looks at me, looks
scared. There's a howl, one of Twig's howls,
building in my throat. Not here.
Not now.
       Shaking
like an old man, I reach over the bed
for the other side of the sheet

and cover my sister's face.

Back in the Family Room,

I walk over to Mom,
stoop, and put my arms around her.
Might as well hug a rag-doll.

She stands up. I let go.

Same corridor. Same nurse at the desk.
She doesn't look up
from her monitor.
                A female cop
and a heavy-set guy who's been crying
are standing near the exit.
He ducks his head when he sees us.

Once we're outside,
Dad says, "Local corporal.
The guy's the driver
of the truck. I spoke to him.
Came over the hill and
there she was.
Decent fellow. All broken up."

Scarcely raining now, although it's still blustery.

We pass the detachment.
Dad drives up the hill.
Mom's neck bent.
Dad grips the wheel.
We top the hill, start
down the other side.

I hope the rain
washed away—

Back home, Mom goes straight to their room.
Dad follows.
I go upstairs,
take the extra key out of my drawer,
and unlock Roxy's door.

Sit on her bed.
Dead hasn't sunk in.
        Any minute she'll storm
through the door and order me out, eyes snapping.

Place is a mess.
        I lean over and pick up
her purple sweater, hold it to my face.
The perfume with the fancy French name
she bought on sale at the drugstore,
it fills my head with Roxy.

I wake up

early
as if
it's a school day
not
Saturday
lie there
what a god-
awful dream
I'm cold
like she's
touching
my skin
I'll never
see my sister
again
never
so heavy
on my chest
I can't
breathe

Someone's made coffee.

Dad's at the table
in his old flannel shirt.
Mom's staring out the window.

I put my hand
on her shoulder.
She tenses.
"Mom?"

Dad says, his voice too loud,
"Coral, I want to make the coffin myself."

She bows her head.
"How *could* you, Bertram?"

"I have to," he says. "Nix,
will you help me?"
His eyes bloodshot, pleading.

"Yes," I say.
Knot in my belly.

He drains his mug.
"Let's get started."
I pour a coffee and follow him
to the workshop.

Chase texts

anything I can do
let me know

I text *thx*

and wish I could forget
the Iron Maiden CD
on top of the pile
on my bureau—yellow-eyed
Eddie-the-skeleton
whipping his red-eyed
black horses. *Death*
on the Road. We're finishing
the dovetails. Handmade,
not with the router,
even though time
is short.
After he cut himself
twice, Dad
left me to chisel the waste.

A car door slams.
Dad looks out the window

and lets the corporal in.
Navy pants with a yellow stripe,
name tag on her shirt.
McTaggart.
Bare head. Gun
on her hip.

"Mr. Humbolt...Nixon," she says. "I need to talk to you, sir."
"Nix can stay," Dad says.
"Your wife? Should she be here?"
"She's lying down."

The corporal starts talking.
Abnormal weather conditions.
Truck below the speed limit.
Roxanne hit in the middle of the road.
Blood alcohol 0.14.

Dad gives a strangled gasp.
"I'm so sorry, sir," the corporal says.
She does look sorry. Human,
not like the cops on TV.

Roxy was drunk.

Too late for Dad to ground her now.

The corporal holds out a bulky envelope.
"The relevant documents are inside.
Also her jewelry, iPhone, and wallet."
She adds apologetically, "Roxanne was wearing
earbuds at the time of the accident."

Who was she listening to? Not Iron Maiden.
The Gaslight Anthem? Deadmau5?

Dad stares at the envelope,
                hands at his sides.
I take it from her, lay it on the bench.
A business card stapled to one corner.

"We're conducting an investigation
into her whereabouts that night, Mr. Humbolt.

If you have any questions or concerns,
please feel free to contact me at any time."

Dad nods.
She and I look at each other.
Then she leaves.

Dad picks up a chisel, puts it back down.
"I never knew Roxy to take a drink," he says.

All weekend, neighbors

deliver casseroles, home-baked rolls, salads, pies.
Thing is, we're not hungry.

Sorry for your trouble...
Sorry for your loss...

Early Sunday morning

before Dad and me start work
on the coffin,
and late Sunday evening
when I'm so tired
I don't know
what to do with myself,
I go into Roxy's room.
I just sit there.
Or I tidy up a bit, turfing stuff
she wouldn't have left lying around
if she'd known.

                                    * * *

I tried turning on Xbox.
Return to checkpoint.
Respawn.

Right.

The wake's Tuesday

at Downton's Funeral Parlor.

We load the coffin on Dad's truck
Monday afternoon.
Oiled birch, beveled lid,
fancy brass handles. Dad lined it
with white satin left over
from Aunt Gerd's niece's
wedding dress. All weekend,
we worked side by side,
neither of us
mentioning Roxy's name.

The highway to St. Jerrold
is dry. Near the top of the hill,
thick black skid marks.

* * *

The wake. Endless
people. Mom white-faced,
Dad in a suit.
If more person uses the word *passed*
I'll plough them.
Chase and Blue,
her eyes wet,
his handshake like
something to hold
onto. Loren, who
kisses my cheek,

her perfume
spring flowers
not heavy-duty
like Roxy's.
Roxy...I grip the nearest
elbow, which belongs to
Blue. She doesn't even wince.
Kendel mumbles,
"Sorry, Nix," and
I can tell he means it.
Our English teacher
doesn't say anything,
just shakes my hand.
Too many others
want to tell me stories
about Roxy, give me back
parts of her I never had.
Suzie, who had the party
Friday night, she
isn't at the wake.
Neither is Bryan Sykes.

After supper

I can't stand being in the house. So
I go for a walk on the barrens.

Bruised clouds over the Three Brides.
Sunset bleeding into the ponds.

* * *

Even though it makes me feel guilty as sin
when my sister's not even buried,

I miss Twig out here,
her skinny legs
her furry, damp-dog smell.

Nix, look after your sister.

I knew Roxy had been into the booze because I'm the one
who sobered her up.

She told me she'd learned her lesson about those
pretty pink coolers,
but I shouldn't have believed one word she said.

I tried to warn her about Kristen. Roxy didn't listen because
I didn't have the guts to tell her flatout what I saw.
Bryan's hand on Kristen's neck. Bryan's lips on her cheek.

I knew Roxy was going after him Friday night
and I knew it was hopeless,
so why did I let her go? On her own. To face that crowd.
I should've crashed the party. Looked after her, protected her
like a brother's supposed to.

If Dad had seen how drunk she was that weekend,
he'd have put an end to it. *Politician's son*
wouldn't cut any wood with Dad.
Ditto if Mom had known Roxy stayed at Bryan's overnight.

You're dumber than dirt...too late to say I'm sorry.
I sat in my room—my safe little room—
listening to her get ready for the party.

Why didn't I walk across the hall, tap on her door,
and thank her for suggesting the video,
for caring about Twig?

Why didn't I say good-bye.

The spray of pink roses

on the coffin is from Mom, Dad, and me.
Roxy would've preferred those dark red ones
that are almost black in the center.

"On the Old Rugged Cross,"
gloomiest hymn in the book.

Mr. Gansy, who drives our school bus,
stands stiff as a veteran on parade.
Mrs. Gansy's hat like a pie plate
with a geranium on top.

No sign of Suzie, Bryan, or Kristen.
The rest of the school
and all the teachers are here.

Mom weeping, Dad's arm around her,
as we follow the coffin down the aisle.
Like a wedding procession. Except it's not.

I stare straight ahead.

The burial is in the old cemetery in Bullbirds Cove.
Gulls wailing, playful little waves, sun
blaring from a cloudless sky. The family
lined up on bright green AstroTurf.

Aunt Gerd sobs out loud. I hold myself rigid.
With the pink roses on top,
the coffin me and Dad made is lowered into the hole.
The minister lobs a chunk of clay on top.

I should've put Fearce in with her.

Everyone troops to our place afterward, where
the church ladies have provided a lunch.
The smell of Mrs. Godsell's asparagus rolls
makes me feel sick.

Chase and Loren stick close. Blue, too.

Finally, they all go home.

* * *

I walk to the landwash, sit on a rock
and listen to the waves. I've listened to them

all my life. They're part of the silence.
A wave curves up, light

shining through it, clear blue green,
not like any other color I ever saw.

Did Dad—the son and grandson of
fishermen—want to open her coffin,

ballast her with granite, carry her
on board Joe Godsell's skiff, and

in the currents off Bullet Reef where
eiders swim, slide her into the sea...

Dad's alone

in the kitchen, propped against the sink,
hands wrapped around his mug
as though he's cold. A jar
of instant coffee on the counter. I

didn't know we had any.
Roxy's chair still sitting at the table.
No one knows what to do with it.
He says, "You got money for lunch?"
I nod. He adds, "I made some toast."

If I eat, I'll puke. I pick up a slice. He says,
"Rough on you, going back to school—"
"Gotta go." I yank my jacket off the hook

and hurry down the driveway,
heart pumping worse than at the funeral.
I toss the toast in the ditch.
Was Roxy thrown on those rocks in the ditch

where the cop was shining his flashlight?
The bus pulls up. I sit near the back.

A few minutes later, Chase, Blue, and Loren
climb on. Chase gives me a light punch
on the shoulder, then he and Loren
sit across the aisle. Blue sits next to me,
has the sense not to say anything.

School's divided into kids who have the nerve
to look me in the eye and kids who
edge around me like I'm contagious.

At noon, in the cafeteria, I find Suzie
sitting with Lara and two other girls.
"Suzie," I say, "gotta minute? I'm wondering
about something. Was Bryan Sykes
putting the moves on Kristen
the night of your party?"

Suzie's not the brightest star in the sky.
"He's got the hots for her—
that's what I told the cops

when they came asking questions."
Like it isn't important, I say,
"I bet Roxy didn't take that sitting down."
"She had a major fight with Bryan," Suzie says.
"Is that when she started drinking?"
"*I* didn't give her anything to drink."

"She always did love those pink coolers,"
I say, smooth-tongued as a salesman.
So casual I want to smack her, Lara says,

"She downed three of 'em before
she started on the beer."
Another girl says, "But we never
saw her leave. Honest we didn't."
"Thanks," I say, and walk out of the cafeteria.

I march down the corridor.

Squeak of my sneaks
on the tiles. Dried-up gum and gray fluff
wedged in the crack between the lockers and the floor.

Bryan Sykes—every hair in place—is standing
beside his locker with a buddy of his.
The guy says something.
Bryan grins.
       He sees me.
The grin vanishes. He looks wary, defensive,
maybe even guilty, and what difference

does it make. I knee him into the locker,
lunge for his throat. Fear contorts his face.
Flooded with roaring
exultant rage, I bash his head
on the hard gray metal
once
twice
praying that the louvers are slicing
his scalp open, that blood's running
down his neck, and somewhere a voice
is rasping, "You bastard, you bastard—"

A girl screams and guys are whooping it up
but I don't give a shit I'm
gonna kill the sonofabitch. He gets
his feet under him, shoves me, throws
two fast punches.

I'm rocked on my heels. He kicks me
in the knee. Pain
stabs my leg. I hurl myself at him

hammering his chest, his belly, that fleshy thud
you hear on TV when
his fist

comes from nowhere and I'm
on the floor, him heavy on my chest,
pounding my face.
                    Through a red
haze I flail at his crotch. He makes
a sound between a grunt
and a yelp. I fling him off,
stagger to my feet, and kick him

vicious-hard in the ribs.
He grips my ankle, tugs me
off-balance.
                    I'm seized
from behind. Struggling, I throw
my weight sideways
                    and free one arm,
strike out with an elbow. Chase gasps,
"Nix, quit it!"
The French teacher's
coming on the run, the principal
on his heels. What's the French word for
kill? Sudden silence. The kids fall back.

I catch a glimpse of Blue's face, horrified,
as she worms through the crowd.

Bryan pushes himself upright. I'm two inches
shorter than the guy I was doing my best
to clobber into extinction.

He's gasping for breath. "I'll get you for this."
"You prick."
"*Assez, M'sieur Humbolt!*"
Words pour like acid off my tongue. "Sixteen,
that's how old she was. You let her
get drunk. You screwed her
while it suited you, then dropped her like—"
"That's enough!" the principal says. "Both of you,
come with me. Everyone else, to your classrooms."

My legs are shaking so hard that if Chase lets go
I'll be on my knees. I grip his sleeve.
"I'm not going anywhere with Bryan Sykes."

Chase says, "Mr. Squires, I'll call Nix's father.
He'll drive Nix home."

"He must take Nix to Emergency first.
I'll drive Bryan there myself."
Mr. Squires straightens his tie. "If assault charges are laid,
we'll require medical evidence.
Nix, I'll talk to you tomorrow morning."

I lick blood off my lip. "You tell Bryan Sykes
to go right ahead and lay charges—I'll raise such a stink
his father will be one dead politician."

I'm not going near Emergency.

After Chase uses his cell

to call Dad, I wobble my way outside.
Even my bones hurt. I lean against
the brick wall. My vision's kinda
     blurry.

Chase says, sounding a long ways
from laidback, "You're gonna have a black eye
       and the skin's split
on your nose. Hope it's not busted."

I close both eyes.
Which is when the real pain begins, gnawing
at every nerve. "Thanks for calling Dad,"
I say through a lip fat as
blubber.
      Maybe Mr. Squires
will suspend me. Or—even better—
I'll be expelled. We wait for Dad's truck,
me dabbing my nose and focusing on

not groaning.
       Dad drives into the school yard,
climbs out of the truck. I try to loosen my muscles
enough to stand upright. Through the only eye
that seems to be open, I see terror on his face.
His boots anchor themselves to the pavement.

"It's okay," I say. "I was in a fight.
The other guy looks worse."

Chase says edgily, "Bryan Sykes."
Dad says, "The fellow Roxy was dating."
"Yeah," I say, "the fellow Roxy was dating."

I can see the wheels turning. But all Dad says is,
"Nix, let's get you in the truck. You might need
a couple stitches."
                              I swipe at my cheek, check out
the blood on my fingers. "I'm not going to Emergency."

His shoulders sag. "Yes, you are. Your face
has to be cleaned up before your mother sees it."

He and Chase lever me into the truck.

"I'll see you tomorrow," Chase says.
He closes the truck door
without giving me his usual punch on the arm.
Likely figured enough was enough.

As we drive away

from the school, Dad says,
"Hospital first. Questions later."

Maybe because we're both dreading it,
Emergency isn't so bad. Three stitches
across my nose, ice for my eye
and my knee.
                   I catch sight of myself in a mirror.
"Jeez, Dad, Mom'll freak out."
"You should've thought of that earlier."
"Let's go out the other door. I don't want to lay eyes
on Bryan Sykes."
In the parking lot, Dad puts the key in the ignition,
then turns in his seat to look at me.
"Why'd you wale into him?"

I gaze through the windshield, wondering what part of the truck
hit Roxy. Wondering what kind of sound
the impact made. "Bryan was mouthing off about Roxy...
guess I didn't stop to think."

"You could be nailed with assault."

"I doubt it." Fact is, I don't care.

I don't know

what Dad tells Mom. At supper
she looks at my face, winces, stashes the plates
in the dishwasher, then goes to their bedroom.
Seems like she's living there these days.

What would she do if she knew the truth?
What would Dad do?

Gee, Mom and Dad, did I forget to mention that Roxy
had sex with Bryan the weekend you were away?
And later on, he brought her home drunk?
And that I covered for her both times?

* * *

Shuffling papers on his desk, the principal tells me
that Mr. Sykes won't be laying assault charges.
I can write my finals, but other than that, I'm suspended
for two weeks.

One smart dude, that Mr. Sykes.

* * *

Friday evening
I stay in my room.
A week ago
Roxy was alive.

I never found out the exact time of the accident.

The minutes creep by
until it's midnight.
I know for sure
she was dead by then.

* * *

I spend the weekend gazing out my window
through my good eye, textbooks open
in front of me. In the classroom, I write Social Studies
and French, pen moving from side to side,
from top to bottom. Marks high enough
for exemptions in the rest. Knuckles still sore.

I catch sight of Bryan near the main door. His bruises,
like mine, match our school colors—burgundy and yellow.

Some of the girls
are looking at me with new eyes. I might be spaced out
but I'm not blind.

Kendel Greene stops me in the corridor, draping
an arm over my shoulders. "Hey there, Nix."
I step away so his arm drops to his side. "Bugger off."

Respect from the likes of Kendel Green?
I'd have to be on my beam ends.

* * *

Blue, sitting alone in the cafeteria,
her nose buried
in a book.
          Loren sits down
beside her. Easy to see
they like each other. I look away.

* * *

No word from the corporal. Or if there is,
Dad's keeping it to himself.

* * *

I make the picture frame for Loren's mother.
Chisel, saw, and sandpaper, they used to take me
out of myself.

Chase picks up the frame,
hangs around for a while. It's like he knows
there's nothing to say
so he doesn't bother trying. Kind of restful.

* * *

Dad and me have taken over the laundry,
the vacuuming, and the dishes. We're still eating
casseroles from the freezer. Day after day
we sit in the kitchen, three of us picking
at our food, Roxy the fourth one at the table.

* * *

From here to St. Jerrold,
        dandelions
        are blooming
        along the ditches
like the yellow suns my sister Roxanne used to paint.

The same year Mom gave Roxy

the polar bear, she gave me a big brown bear
with round shoulders, his eyes
half-asleep. I called him Bandit.
When I was ten, Kevin Godsell
came to pick up his kid brother's
homework. Mom sent him upstairs
to my room.
      Next day, everyone at school
knew I kept a stuffed bear
on my bed. I waited until
Mom was at the store and buried Bandit
in the garbage. Spaghetti
slime. Splintered glass.
All these years, Roxy
has hung onto Fearce. Girls are softer
and tougher than guys.
           I bring Fearce
into my room and sit him on the bureau.

Fearce doesn't keep

the nightmares away. Fanged
sea monsters, Roxy
mangled on Bullet Reef, *rescue me...*
I shower, pad downstairs. Maybe
coffee will help.
                    Mom's
sitting at the table. Sitting
like a corpse. "Morning," I say.
She gives me blank look,
which is all I get these days.
"Nixon," I say, "I'm your son, Nixon."
She lines up her juice glass
with her coffee mug,
and stands up.
Dad stands up too.
He tries to put his arms around her.
"Please don't, Bertram...please."
"Coral, I need—"
"When you touch me, I feel like I'm going to fly apart—
break into a thousand pieces."
                    Dad's face,
hurt piled on hurt.

We're all flying apart, Mom, or hadn't you noticed?

Mom hurries to the bedroom.
Dad stands like a stump.
I reach for the Cheerios.

Dad's taken Mom to the doctor

to get a prescription for sleeping pills.
I walk to our box for the mail.

A small parcel is stuffed inside, from a bookstore
in Maryland. It's addressed to:

> *Roxanne Humbolt.*

I walk home, kicking at the dandelions, grinding
their yellow faces into the dirt.

In my room I open the parcel, tape
sticking to my fingers, and pull out the book.
A brown and white mutt on the cover.
How to Care for Your Adopted Dog.

Something way beyond a sob bursts from my chest.
Then another, and another, until I can't

shove them down, I can't stop them, they're
crowding their way out, tears streaming

down my face, me gasping and gulping
for breath, and all I want is for her to walk

in the door, Roxy at her total worst, and
I'd throw my arms around her and never let go.

* * *

My throat's raw when I finally quit, although
little shudders and hiccups keep forcing their way up.

I splash cold water on my face, and remember
how I held her head under the tap.

* * *

After checking the date on the invoice,
I think backward. She ordered the book
the day Dad dragged Twig over to Swiff's truck.
The day she was so nice to me.
The day I hugged her.

She must've believed Twig would end up
living with us. No wonder she was pissed
that I was sitting on my butt
instead of rescuing
my dog.

I clear away the supper dishes.

Mom goes to her room.
Dad goes to the workshop.
He's behind in his orders.

In the workshop, he's gluing oak boards
for a drop-leaf table.
I walk up to him, stand there.

"Dad, I'm going to Sharkey Bay.
To get evidence Arnie's mistreating the dog."

He tightens the jaws of the clamp, slowly, deliberately.
"How you gonna get there?"

"You sent Twig back to Arnie's—you'll drive me.
Tomorrow morning. Before you start work."

"You're pushing your luck."

"While I'm there, I might ask some of the locals
about my grandparents."

His fingers jerk on the handle.

"The old lady who gave me and Twig a drive
told I'm the spitting image
of Neil Ardrich.
             Him and his wife Elaine
used to live in Sharkey Bay. When they died in a fire
thirty-three years ago, their little girl was seven.
They were Mom's parents, weren't they?"

"You've got it all worked out," Dad says.

"I'm good at math."

Dad looks at me. Through me.
"Roxy wanted you to have that dog.
But I didn't listen to her because my mind was made up.
I'll drive you first thing tomorrow. And I'll square it
with your mother."

His eyes focus on me.
"Don't let on to her that you know about her parents.
　　　This is no time to dig up old history."
"How come you never told me—wasn't it worth mentioning?"

"Not my story to tell." Dad picks up the glue.
Man, can he kill a conversation.

"Want help with the mortises?" I say.

The rest of the evening we work in silence,
side by side.

When we drive up Arnie's road

the sun's just over the trees.
His truck isn't parked outside his house.
Twig doesn't even look up.

After Dad turns around, he stops
on the side of the road. "All set?"
"Yeah...I'll hang around all day."
"I'll be back at dusk. Be careful, Son—
your mother would never forgive me
if anything happened to you."
"Don't you start smothering me!"
"That the way you see it?"
"I've got my phone."
         Has he guessed
how much I don't want to do this?
"The video was Roxy's idea," I say.
He reaches over and ruffles my hair.
I give him one of Chase's shoulder-jabs
and climb out of the truck.
         He drives away.
I slink up the road to Arnie's.

Twig's nose is on her paws and her eyes are closed.
I creep nearer, trying
not to dislodge the smallest stone.
Ducking behind a pile of lumber, I settle down.

Once Arnie's back and in the house,
I'll show myself to Twig.
She'll raise hell. I'm counting on it.

Then, from behind my pile of lumber,
I'll see how Arnie deals.

The day drags on.
Minute by minute.
Hour by hour.
Hang in there, bro...

When it's too dark to video,
I hear a truck coming.
      Dad's truck, not Arnie's.
Bent low, I creep back down the road
and climb in the truck.
"Arnie never came home," I say.

Same deal next morning, except

Dad drops me at the side of the highway.
He says, "I have three deliveries
south of here—Port au Choix and River of Ponds.
I want you to call me
            soon as you're done.
If you have to stay all day,
I'll come back this evening."
"Thanks, Dad."
                    I mean it
and he knows I mean it.

Like yesterday, I sneak up the road.
Arnie's truck, spattered with mud, is parked in the driveway.
Venetian blinds tight shut in the upstairs windows.

I tuck myself behind the pile of lumber,
take out my phone and turn it on.

Pulse racing, I raise my head
and call, none too loud, "Twig...Twig."
She springs to her feet, straining
at the chain, whining.
"Twig..."
The whines turn to barks. Loud barks.
The blinds jerk.

Arnie charges out the front door in jeans
and a black t-shirt. "Shut up!"
But Twig's caught my scent and nothing's
                    gonna shut her up.

Arnie hauls his leather belt out of his waistband.
I aim the phone,
hands resting on an end of wood,
and click on the video function.
Eyes trained on the screen
where the seconds show in white.

0.03, 0.07, 0.11...he's
beating her and the only thing I can do
is hold the phone
and keep it in focus.
0.14, 0.17...snap of leather
against her fur. The sounds
Twig's making—whimpers
and yelps that run together
that turn into crying—
I can't stand it
and I do
and at 0.22, Arnie stops.

I turn the video function off.
He's breathing hard. Twig's
on her back,
shivering like she's got the flu.

You ever hate someone
so deep
you wish they'd drop dead right in front of you?

He goes inside. I duck down,
knot my fingers until they're steady,
then replay the video.
I got it all, sounds included.

Hunkered behind the lumber—

every knothole memorized—
I listen to Twig
drag herself back to her kennel.

She knows I'm still here.

* * *

Mid-morning, dirt spitting
from his tires, Arnie takes off down the road.
I call Dad, who's heading north
from Port au Choix.

Twig's cowering at the back of the kennel.
"It's okay," I whisper. "This time,
        you're never coming back here.
Never. I promise."

I clip on her leash.
She braces her haunches.
Very carefully I tug her toward me
and lift her in my arms.
She whimpers.

I lug her down the road. Good thing
                        she's skinny.
Sun's up. Mosquitoes out. Sweat
trickling down my face.
                Ears wide
for the sound of Arnie's truck.

I should've told Dad I'd wait for him

in the clump of trees and shrubs
across from the two empty houses
on Arnie's road. But isn't that
the first place Arnie would look?

By the time we reach the highway
my shoulders are cramped.
I put Twig down
and straighten, panting.
Paved road feels safer.

"Okay, Twig, can you manage on your own?"
I say in a voice that's not exactly alpha.
"Walk, girl...walk."

We go slow. She's hurting.

I'm hoping Dad—for once—
will break the speed limit.

A black Dodge truck

approaches the stop sign
on the road leading out of Sharkey Bay.
Arnie checks the traffic both ways.
Sees us. Whips
onto the highway in a spurt of gravel and
                                        heads right for us.
Dropping the leash, I point to the ditch. *"Go! Lie down!"*

Twig sidles into the ditch. Arnie swerves
onto the opposite shoulder. Four steps
take me to the middle of the highway.
Arnie jumps down from his truck, slaps
the door shut, swaggers toward me.
"You're gonna wish you'd stayed home," he says. Knuckles
                                        like pork hocks.
I'm so scared, I got nowhere to go
            but crazy.
I straddle the yellow line, fists clenched.
"My dad's on his way—you touch me, he'll kill you."
"You ain't keeping my goddamn dog."

A car's speeding toward us.
Arnie grabs for me. I duck.
The car brakes fast. Red Acura.
I shout, "Call 911!"
Arnie seizes me by the arm and swings me around like
I'm Twig-size. Barrens, road, houses
whirl past. My jeans
scrape the pavement. I head-butt
his zipper. He belts me.

Frig, if he's wrecked my stitches—
      I'm pounding
any part of him I can reach, when Twig
                              leaps up
and latches onto his leg.
He bellows.
The Acura guy is out of his car,
running toward us. Arnie shakes Twig off,
yanks me upright, cracks me across the ear.
My head rings. A truck
screeches to a halt.

Dad's voice. "Let go of my son."

Now that's alpha.
Arnie lets go.

"Twig," I gasp, "sit."
She quits snarling. But she's not sitting down
for me or anyone else.

We all hear the wail of a siren, cop car
zooming closer in a dazzle
of red and blue.
More action than a shoot-out in *True Grit*.

Corporal McTaggart strides toward us, hand
on her baton. Arnie stands gob-smacked,
like he's been tasered.
Laughter crackles in my chest.

She takes the names of all the witnesses.
I get my voice under control and tell her
about Twig. She watches the video.
Before she impounds my phone,

I pass it to Dad. His face set,
he watches the clip. "I'm real sorry
I sent the dog back there."

The corporal charges Arnie with animal cruelty
and assault. I thank the Acura driver
for calling 911. He's visiting from Nova Scotia.
Right, Nix, do your bit for tourism.

Still in alpha mode, Dad says to the corporal,
                    "We're gonna adopt Twig."
"The shelter in St. Jerrold is full, sir,
so you can take the dog home with you now.
But please don't remove her from the area."

Dad nods.
After she orders Arnie to Emergency
to have the bite cleaned up—I hope
they stick him with twenty blunt needles—
she makes short work
of the traffic jam. We drive off, Twig
at my feet,
me stroking her head, gently,
over and over again.

"You arrived just in time, Dad."
"Don't ever tell your mother Arnie hit you."
Then he reaches over
and rests his hand on my knee.

We turn into our driveway.

Tucked under the eaves of the workshop,
　　　where it'll be shaded
in summer, is a brand-new kennel.

Its shingled roof and cedar clapboard
　　　waver in my vision.
"How'd you know for sure I'd be bringing Twig back?"
"You had Arnie tagged from the start."
"But you're behind in your orders."

"Yeah," Dad says, his grin
almost like old times. "Only four days
before you're in school again. I'm gonna
work your butt off, buddy."

My tongue's so ready to unload
all the shit
I've been carrying around—
pink coolers
Blond Streaks
dumber than dirt.

"Will Mom be okay with us having a dog?"
"Yeah...she'll be okay."

I'm planing an oak board when

Dad lays his chisel on the bench. "There's things
I told your mom that I should've told you, Nix."
My hand tightens on the knob. "Yeah?"

"Week after the funeral,
I went to see Suzie's parents.
        That Friday night,
they were out of town. Cops
have charged them with supplying alcohol
to minors. *Fair enough*, I said to them.

"Next, I stopped off at Bryan's place.
Told his parents what I thought of their son,
who let my daughter start out
on foot in the rain
after she'd been drinking."

His callused thumb rubs the smooth oak
                          . with the grain,
then against it.

"Next day, I talked to the corporal.
Roxy was in with a wild crowd."

I search for something—anything—to fill the silence.
"What did Mom say?"

He picks up the chisel,
looks at it as if he's not sure
what it is. "Not a damn thing."

I need carbs

before I hit the sack. There aren't any homemade cookies.
Mom's quit acting like a mom
in that department too.

By the kitchen door, I stop. Dad's talking.
"Maybe you should see the psychologist
in St. Jerrold, Coral. Doc said he was decent."
"I don't want to."
"I'd go with you."
"How could I talk to someone who's being paid
to listen to me? Anyway,
what would I say? There's nothing
to say."
"I miss you," Dad says hoarsely. "You
and Roxy."
"I can't help you...I'm sorry."

I back up.
I'm sick of Mom acting like she's the only one
who misses Roxy. Sick of Dad
treating her as if she's made of crystal
when he's the one who looks like he'll shatter—

anger comes easy when it's
Mom
Bryan
Arnie
Suzie
even Dad.

But when it's Roxy...seems like I can't...

alive
       she was always on my case
and us yelling at each other was part of our daily routine—
       dead
she's ruining our lives—
enough to piss anyone off—

that chunk of dirt the minister lobbed
in the hole, the small thud when it landed
on the lid—did I lob my anger
underground so it could keep her
warm, leaving me
with this echo in my head, this faraway echo
of a brother yelling at a sister who's yelling
at a brother who—even though
pissed has vanished even though *sister*
has vanished—doesn't know

how to stop
being a brother.

Aunt Gerd takes Mom

shopping. Dad's in the workshop.
I sneak into their room, go through every drawer
in the dresser and bureau, searching for—what?
                    Two missing grandparents?

I pull out the fire-proof safe
Dad keeps under the bed.
The key is in Mom's jewelry box.
I shuffle through the papers.
Will. Insurance policies.
Birth certificates for me and Roxy.
A new envelope. Roxy's
death certificate. *Shitshitshit.*

                    * * *

Later that afternoon, while Dad's
doing a delivery, I check his workshop desk.
Everything neatly labeled and filed.
In the bottom left-hand drawer, I come across
a worn white envelope, the flap stuck down
        with tape that's yellowed
and brittle. I slide out the contents.

Mom and Dad's marriage certificate.
Bertram Whelan Humbolt and Coral Ardrich.

A legal agreement that Silas and Martha Josey
of Cap d'Argent will foster Coral Ardrich
until her eighteenth birthday.

A termination of that agreement
while Mom was only seventeen.

Underneath are two photographs.
A good-looking guy with a cowlick,
one arm around a woman
who resembles Mom.
His other arm holds their little girl.

In the second photo,
wearing a jacket that's too big for her,
a girl of about seven
stands between a man and woman
who look like they wouldn't smile if
they were released from death row.
The girl is Mom. Her face a misery.
But that's not what makes my fingers shake.

She's standing beside a small wooden table.
It has tapered legs and a drawer with a knob.

Funny time to remember
how Mom always wrings the dishcloth
like she's choking someone.

Twig sleeps on my bed at night

where she farts and snores.
We're back to walking the barrens.
      Chuckley pear in bloom. Wildflowers
a purple mist around the ponds,
birds singing their fool heads off.
          Only yellow sun
is in the sky.

* * *

No use asking Dad about the photos.
Even though Chase drops by
every day—can't seem to talk to him either.

* * *

If I see Blue on the barrens, I angle the other way.
There's this dead
weight sitting on me
day and night and I'm not sleeping any too good
because of the nightmares

and blabbing all this crap
to Blue won't make it
go away.

Back in school, nothing's changed

including the mess in my locker.
As I'm sorting the books,
     from the corner of my eye
I see Chase pin Loren to the wall
and kiss her like they're parked
in his old Chevy under a blanket of stars.

The desperate need for her to smile at me
the way she smiles at Chase—it's gone.
Not sure why. Or how.

It's neat they're so tight,
     her and Chase.
I dust off my French text.

Past tense of *je t'aime*.

I'm the only one

in the guys' washroom. I flush
the urinal—janitor goes rabid if you don't—
and wash my hands.
                              It's quiet in here. I could just
stay here until—the door opens.
Bryan says, "Nixon. Heard you were back."
Cyril Watson close on his heels.
No place to hide.
                              Cyril thrusts me
against the wall, my head bashing the tiles
so hard I see three Bryans. One of 'em
                    cracks me across the cheekbone
then Cyril fastens his big hand
over my face so I can't breathe
and Bryan says, "Move out of the way, Cy, so I can kick him
where it hurts."
I can't even struggle
        and I'm running outta air
and that's when
the door bangs open and Kendel Green's
foghorn voice says, "You guys better take a hike.
                              Hansen's on your tail."
Cyril drops his hand.
I heave in oxygen.
        Hansen.
        Math teacher.
        Built like Cyril
        but with brains.
Bryan says sharply, "C'mon, Cy."

Cyril brings up his knee but I've got the wit
to throw myself sideways and
            he thunks my thigh.
With a ferocious smile Bryan says, "We're not
done with you, Nixon,"
and walks out the door casual as if he just had
a good pee. Cyril lumbers after him.

I say, voice shaky, "You're on *my* side, Kendel?"

Kendel rubs his neck. "That day
in the cafeteria, me asking
if Roxy was still screwing Bryan—
and a month later she's dead. Like, *dead*."

"You were at the wake.
You said you were sorry."

"Sorry she was dead.
Sorry I was such a shit.
Sorry for the whole stinkin' world...
I dunno, Nix."

"Well...thanks."
"No prob, man."

A headache's agitating behind my eyes.
We walk out into the corridor.
Kendel winks at me. "Guess Hansen did a bunk."

A nor'easter drives rain over Seven Days Work,

and pretty soon Twig's coat is sticking to her ribs, my hair
plastered to my scalp.
        I can handle Bryan,
          but not Bryan plus Cyril.
So do I run to Chase for help? Enlist him
and the whole goddamn hockey team?
Or do I hire Hansen as my personal bodyguard?

I plunk down on a rock, rest my wet face
on my hands.
        Rain splats
my yellow slicker. My jeans
turn dark, clinging to my legs.
If I had any sense, I'd go home.

Twig wuffs.
My head rears up.
Blue.
Beside a clump of junipers.
Watching me.

I'm on my feet, shoulders hunched. "Spying on me?"
"No!"
"Sure looks that way."
She chews her lip, her soft lip. "I just wish I could help, that's all."
"I don't need your help."

There's one of those pauses that's nanoseconds
but drags its heels until you want to scream.
If I told her about Roxy and the pink coolers—just blurted it out—

Rain trickles down my cheeks.

She says stiffly, "A golden eagle's been reported near here.
That's what I was looking for. Not you."

"Oh. Sorry."
She walks past me.
I grab her elbow.
She looks back over her shoulder.
I let go.
"Be careful," I say. "The roots are slippery."

As I'm hanging my slicker on the peg,

Twig dashes into the kitchen.
Mom's stationed by the stove. "Look at the mud
            your dog tracked in!"
"Don't know why *you're* complaining—Dad and me
do all the housework."
"Don't use that tone of voice with me."
"So you *are* alive," I sneer. "Wow. Blow up the balloons."
"Alive," she repeats. She looks like victim
and sniper all in one.

"Neil and Elaine Ardrich," I say. "You ever
planning on telling me about them?"

She pales, cramping her fingers
around the handle of the kettle. "How do you know...
            your father told you, didn't he?"
"Oh sure, let's blame Dad. Dad didn't tell me.
An old lady in Sharkey Bay told me. A stranger. A
total stranger. Nice way
to learn about your grandparents, hey, Mom?"
"I-I don't—"
"Don't you think it's time you started letting me in on stuff
that's important? Treating me like an adult?"
"I would if you behaved like one!"
"What a load of *crap*."

Which is when Dad walks in the door.
"Nix! Don't use that word to your mother."
"Like she's never heard it before?"
Mom furious

is better than
Mom absent,
doesn't he get it—
"You want me to behave like an adult?
Adults tell the truth, right?
So why don't I do just that.
I knew Roxy drank. She got drunk
right here at the kitchen table
when she was twelve.
And after one of her dates with Bryan
she came home loaded.
I hid her in the workshop,
sobered her up—
it was the night Backstrom walloped
the Penguins. I didn't tell you. Either one of you."

Mom's gone pale.
Dad's face like stone.

But I'm not finished. "The weekend you were in St. John's,
she stayed overnight at Bryan's.
Twice. I covered for her then, too.
If it wasn't for me, you'd have given Bryan the boot
and she'd still be alive—
it's all my fault. The whole damn thing."

Feet like slabs of ice. Wet hair, wet jeans, skin cold as Roxy's.

Mom says, "You lied to me when I phoned that weekend."
"I sure did."

"It wasn't all your fault," Mom says. "Your father
was much too strict. Too hard on her."

Dad gasps.

I've heard of dead silence, who hasn't.
This silence is alive, crawling with—
Dad says in a voice with no feeling to it,
"You were too protective of her, Coral. Hovering
                    over every move she made—"
"You're saying *I'm* responsible?"
"I'm saying we all made mistakes."
"Speak for yourself!"

The heels of Mom's shoes
hit the floor like gunshots.
Their bedroom door slams.
Dad stands there like
he took a bullet in the chest.

"Dad?" I say.

"I better go after her."
He shuffles out of the kitchen.

Upstairs, I plunk myself down on my sister's bed.

Okay, Rox, now what do I do?

It's four weeks

and time is still
out of whack.
      A few seconds when I can't believe—and I mean
can't—that she's dead,
                             they last forever.

Then a whole day goes by
and I realize I don't have a clue what I've been doing
from one hour to the next.

Thick fog.

Twig and me are walking the barrens—
she won't get lost. Everything's dissolved to

nothing. The silence full of muffled
sounds. Twig dives under a shrub, hauls out

a dead rabbit. Tatters of skin,
tidy rows of teeth. Scraps

of dark flesh clinging to the bones.
She crunches the skull, puts one paw

on the front leg and tugs at the spine.
In my ear a voice says, *Gross...eeeuw.*

Joy rockets through me. It's all been a nightmare—
I've woken up—she's right behind me, neon-pink hair,

face squinched, *Nix...so totally disgusting!*
Pulse racing, I pivot.

Fog.
Snap of bone.

Kendel must've yapped to the whole school

about Cyril, Bryan, and the guys' washroom.
Chase tells me one of the Scoters
will be trailing me wherever I go.
                              Bryan gives me
filthy looks. Cyril gets in a couple of good kicks, but
one day when he elbows me into the cafeteria door
three defence players surround him
quick as if they're on skates.
                              He backs off.
One of life's sweet moments.
"Thanks, guys," I say, they high-five,
and I order mac cheese.

                    * * *

School ends. My summer job begins.
Same as last year, Dad pays me minimum wage
for prep and clean-up. Humbolt & Son.
Also, I make picture frames, cutting boards
and small benches for gift shops along the shore.

Dad's gone silent. Like, total.
Doesn't refer to my confession,
never mentions Roxy's name.
              I was hoping
this summer would be more like
two's tougher than one.
Humbolt & Humbolt.

June turns into July and July keeps going,

day after day. Sometimes it rains, the drops making
craters in the puddles. Sometimes it's sunny,
the gulf sparking like gunfire.

Chase coaches summer hockey
in Corner Brook for a week, then flies to Vermont
for two weeks of hockey school.

It occurs to me he's my only friend.
Unless you count Kendel.

Blue's leading nature walks at a kids' camp.
So I don't have to worry
about bumping into her on the barrens,
which is where I go most every day.

> Stuff doesn't feel as heavy
> out there. All that blue sky.
> Mountains so old they're beyond
> caring.

To keep Dad company in front of the TV,
now Mom's given up on it, I watch the news
every night. People dying all the time,
mud slides, mine disasters, Modern Warfare
in countries I'd have a hard time locating on a real map.

I'm gluing and clamping

picture frames one after the other,
and I'm thinking how I've dovetailed
                        guilt to grief—
the whole point of dovetails being
it takes a sledgehammer
to break the joint—
                when Blue
texts me. Wants me to make some roosting boxes.

Half an hour later, she arrives with the plans.
"Hi there," she says, voice not giving anything away.

Plain green t-shirt, mud-brown shorts.
She needs Roxy.

Not for her hair, though.
                        Or
her eyes. They make me feel like
I've jumped in the ocean—that sudden
shock, skin tingling.

Nice legs, too. Scratched up
from walking the barrens.

"Hi," I say.
I search the cavities in my brain.
"How did the nature walks go?"

As she describes kids falling
into brooks, falling

out of canoes, screeching
because they saw a leech,
her voice warms.
It all sounds so normal.

Blue takes a scrap of paper out of her pocket,

writes a name on it with a stubby pencil, and passes it to me.
Guiseppe Penone.
      "He works with wood," she says. "Mom came across him
when she was surfing Toronto art galleries.
Google him sometime."

I've had enough of picture frames.
"Want to go out on the barrens?" I say.

"Sure—there's something I'd like you to see."

My favorite time on the barrens is evening,
when the light's golden
and the ponds look polished.
                        We hike
to a gully with a few scruffy trees,
where we hunker down, Twig at my feet.
Blue peers through her binoculars, then passes them to me.
"Third tree from the left, near the top."

Takes me a couple seconds because I don't know
what I'm looking for.
                  Flitting
from branch to branch, never
still, is a bird, a little flare
of a bird, dandelion-
yellow, yellow
as the suns Roxanne
used to paint.

The bird darts closer to the ground, vanishes
among the shrubs.
                    Loss
bends me forward, arms wrapped
around my ribs to hold it in.

Light as a bird, Blue's hand rests
on my shoulder. Under my closed lids,
specks of yellow, dancing.
                          If only
I could let it all pour out. But my throat's locked
and those ugly sounds are me, breathing.

When I finally lift my head, the yellow bird
is back on the same tree. I fumble for words.
"I gotta pay more attention when I'm out here."

Blue rambles on about yellow warblers for a while,
then she says, "I saw Bryan at Tims the other day.
With a different girl, not Kristen."
"That figures."
"You can talk to me anytime, Nix...I don't gossip
            and I wouldn't tell Chase."
"There's nothing to talk about."
"I guess I'm...your feelings,
that's what I mean. My dad plays his fiddle, Mom
tosses color around, and I—"
"My sister already told me I live my life
in a box. I don't need you
                  dealing the same crap."
"Your woodwork's beautiful!
It's the rest of you I'm worried about."

I try to stop myself—I swear I do.
But it's like I'm spewing vomit. "Nobody asked you
to worry about me."
"If you'd only— "
"You don't know the first thing about it! You've still got
Chase. Your mom hasn't disappeared
off the face of the earth. Your dad
doesn't look like someone stuck a screwdriver
                              through his heart."
"Nix, I—"
"Roxy's gone. Dead and buried.
What part of that don't you get? Leave me
alone, will you? Just leave me alone."
"Fine," she says, loops her binoculars
around her neck and walks away.

I glue my feet to the ground
so I won't run after her.

Twig's ears droop.

I'm not sure I'll make it home,
I'm so frigging tired.

In the middle of the night

I turn on my laptop and Google Guiseppe Penone
—what is he, bit player in *The Godfather?*

Photo of a stocky, ordinary-looking guy
wearing faded denim
and glasses. Needs a shave.

Photo of a long gallery, arc
of wooden beams from floor to ceiling and
light. So much light.

The third photo—there's a huge tree trunk
standing in the center of the gallery—

this Penone guy has cut open
the tree's heart,
and in the hollow
he's carved
a sapling
> straight
> smooth
> strong
> its branches
> growing into the trunk
> yet
> freed from the trunk
as if it's always been there,
waiting
for him to find it.

I sit there
like I've been shot.

Chase comes home from hockey school.

He suggests we start running with Twig
so he can stay in shape for fall.

"Running," I say.
"You know, faster than a jog, slower than a sprint."
"I know what running is."
It's taking to your heels
when you see a black half-ton.

"You've just come back from hockey school," I say,
"you could run circles around me."
"You'll do fine."

Twig will enjoy it.
It'll get me out of the house,
where cutting the tension
would take a band-saw
with a brand-new blade.

It's my sixteenth birthday

and I feel like the bottom
of the birdhouse. *Lice* and *feces*,
to quote Blue, who I'm doing my level best
to forget.

In the workshop, Dad hands me an envelope.
"I took this last winter," he says. "Didn't want
your mother to see it."

I pull out a color photo, 6" x 8".
We'd been playing Skip-bo
and I'd won (dealt so many wild cards,
how could I lose).
Roxy has her arm around me.
We're laughing.

I make a sound between a gasp and a groan.
Dad squeezes my shoulder.
We get to work.

At supper, Mom gives me one of those blank cards
where you write your own message.

Happy Birthday, Nixon,
xo
Mom and Dad

Nixon xo
Roxanne ox
Our family steers away from stuff like *I love you.*

There's money inside the card, for Drivers' Ed.
"Good if you could drive the truck," Dad says.

Not at night in the rain.

He barbecues spareribs for supper.

Mom's baked my favorite lemon cake with buttercream icing.

I help with the dishes.

Then I figure it's okay to escape to my room.

I keep hoping

I won't notice it's Friday again.

We've finished supper and I'm loading
the dishwasher, Mom scraping the plates,
when Dad says, "Ten weeks today."

Water sluices over the plate Mom's holding
                        under the tap.
"Bertram," she says, "I can count."
"Coral, I wish you'd—"
"I've lost my daughter," Mom says
as formally as if she's talking to the Prime Minister.
"This is a great sorrow to me. You must allow me
to cope in my own way."

Carefully she turns off the tap and puts
the wet plate on the counter. Then she starts
weeping into the empty sink.

Dad walks over to her, his steps slow and heavy.
He puts his arms around her. She elbows him
in the ribs. "Don't touch me!"
"You never let me touch you! Not since Roxy died."
"When are you going to listen to me? All I can do
is hold myself together—I can't deal with you as well.
It's too much."

They've forgotten I'm here. Her face
tear-streaked, his stricken.

He says,
        gravel in his throat, "I can't stand it
when you shut me out."

"Mom, this isn't only about you!" My voice
        skids up an octave,
something it hasn't done in years. "We all lost Roxy.
You act like you're the only one
who misses her. You think he doesn't? He was her father."
"Don't start on me," she says.

Her face rigid, bitter...spitting image
of the woman standing by the table, her foster mother
        from Cap d'Argent.

"You never want to hear from me. Roxy
was the smart one, the funny one,
and now you're stuck with your boring son.
You're stuck with Dad, too.
        Try cutting him some slack, why don't you?"
"My marriage is *my* business."
"Coral, stop this!"
"I want both of you to leave me alone."
"Nix is right," Dad says, "it's always about you."

Even in my bedroom, I can hear their voices
                        like hammer blows.
Is an adult just a teenager with a layer of veneer?

I was gonna Google

Guiseppe Penone again
but I type in *divorce* instead, then
statistics, narrow it to
divorce rate after death of a child.

One study: 80-90%
Another study: 12%

How's a guy supposed to make sense of this?
How's a guy supposed to make sense of anything?

If they did divorce, who would I go with?
That's easy. Dad.
Who'd do the cooking?

* * *

Next day, Mom and Dad
are each surrounded by a No Fly Zone.
Guess there wasn't any of the make-up sex
I read about—in detail—in that magazine
I found in Roxy's closet.

Occasionally—

even though I feel like a louse
afterward—I find myself thinking
it's downright peaceful
without Roxy. No bitching.
No red hairs clogging the sink,
no soggy towels draped over the toilet.
No tampons new or used.
I can read *Playboy* or squeeze my zits
without her pounding on the door.
My phone stays where I put it.
I sure don't miss The Gaslight Anthem.
Or Deadmau5.

That word *accident*...

...want to know what I think?
There aren't any accidents.
                              Just endless
chains of cause and effect, going back and back and
back. If the truck driver had refilled his coffee
at Tims...if he'd turned the newspaper over
and read the juicy scandal on the back...if
the woman behind the counter had stopped
to chat but she didn't because she'd had a fight
with her daughter who'd missed winning two million by
two numbers...or if his wife had called and he'd pulled over
except she didn't because their kid had the flu and
she was trying to settle him to sleep and he caught
the flu from the little girl in daycare because he wanted
the red truck not the blue one and she wouldn't let go...

any one of those *ifs* and the truck driver
could've been on a straight stretch
and seen Roxy
in time.

Another thing.
How many accidents
have you avoided
that you'll never know about?

Two minutes earlier...
Thirty seconds later...

The waves on the shore

kind of hypnotize me.
      It's dark, a half-moon
like chips of silver on the swell...

I'm at the far end of the cove,
out of sight of the houses.
Mom and Dad are at Uncle Mort's.
Mom and Uncle Mort will have one glass of gin each.
Dad will drink ginger ale.
Some things never change.

I stand up, stretch. I could work on the roosting boxes
for a while—no time during the day.

Straining my eyes, I clamber over the rocks
toward the houses, then navigate the ditch. Headlights
coming toward me. Too
bright.
      The car stops. Two guys get out,
me still half-blinded...
            Cyril. And Bryan.
Digging my sneaks in the gravel, I leap
for the other ditch. Cyril tackles me
and I'm down, his weight
slamming me into the road.
      Bryan says, "Don't break anything, Cy—
just rough him up. I want to hear him
begging, right, Nixon?"

Fear near to chokes me. Cyril tugs one arm
across my back, jerks it up,
leans on it.
        I bite off a scream.
Bryan says, "We've been following you, buddy.
Convenient you came down here.
Do it again, Cy. Harder."
        The noise coming out of me
is way past screaming. Bryan says, "There's rocks
in the ditch. Let's scrape his face up some."

who told him about Roxy's face

Cyril lifts me by the elbows, drags me
toward the ditch. Granite. Murky water and
            I go berserk
        kicking thrashing twisting
        shoulders like they're torn
from their sockets. One arm free. Flail
at him. A heel hacks my shin. He cinches
my arm. I'm down again,
head down in the ditch, sobbing
            with rage. He jams
my face onto the nearest rock,
presses hard, pulls me back real slow. The sounds I make—
I can't help it, white-hot pain
skin being peeled—
                "Truck's coming! Leave him, Cy."

Cyril's weight, it's off me.
I gotta get outta here.

Staggering, I'm on my feet, bile
sour in my mouth. I stumble
over the rocks in the ditch. The truck

slows down. I wade
through the water.
         Car doors
slam as I slog up the other side.

In a spurt of gravel, a small gray Honda
takes off down the road.
Not the Lexus. Can't use a Lexus
for your dirty work.

The truck speeds up, follows the Honda.
Limping, breath rasping,
I lurch across Wally Budgen's excuse for a lawn.

When I lift my hand to my face, it comes away wet with blood.

No truck in our driveway.

Kitchen empty. I lean on the table. Can't
stop shaking.
                Drops of blood
on the floor and the place mat.
I grope for a cloth under the sink, wet it, bend over
to wipe the tiles.
                Dizziness lands me
on my knees, crouched on all fours like a dumb
animal. Twig's claws skitter down the stairs, then
she's nosing my face, whining.

I push her muzzle away. "Twig, gotta clean up before—"
                      She barks.
Dad's truck pulls up by the house.

Clinging to the nearest chair
I stand up. Too late to run...even if I could.

Mom comes into the kitchen first.
Sees my face.
                Her face white,
she sways on her feet. Dad grabs for her,
his arm around her shoulders. She wraps her arm
around his waist.
        I say muzzily, "Long time
since you guys had a decent hug."

Mom straightens. Fierce as a she-bear,
she says, "Who did that to your face?"

"Fell. On the rocks."
Dad says, and it isn't a question, "Bryan Sykes."

"Bertram, fetch the first-aid kit. Nixon, sit down."

I collapse into the chair. All I want to do
is lay my head on the table and wake up
next month. "Made a mess on the floor."
"The floor will wash."
It's the old Mom speaking. "I've missed you," I mutter
as Dad hurries in with the first-aid kit.

She looks from me to Dad
and back again. Tears spout
from her eyes. She seizes Dad's hand,
bringing it to her wet cheek,
and clutches my shoulder.
"I've missed both of you...I've felt so far away and lonely."
The love in her voice,
                    it hurts my ears.
Dad's smile would light a whole hospital.

I rest the good side
of my face on Mom's arm.

They're both waiting for me

at the kitchen table the next morning.
Holding hands. Like they're the ones who are sixteen.

Mom cleaning my face last night hurt as bad
as anything Cyril did. Chockful of painkillers,
I slept nine hours.

Mom says, "We made a doctor's appointment
this afternoon to check those scrapes."
No point arguing
with that voice.

Dad says quietly, "What happened, Nix?
    Was it Bryan?"
"Bryan and his buddy Cyril."
"We're going to the police," Mom says.
I wince. "I'll talk to Bryan. It won't happen again."
Dad drums his fingers on the table. "We should lay charges.
Scraping up your face like Roxy's—that's cruel."
"I'll talk to both of them. Cyril does what Bryan says."
"If there's talking to be done,
it'll be in a public place. Understood?"
"I get it. No back alleys."
"I think I'll drop into the detachment anyway
and have a chat with the corporal."
"Dad—"
"Yeah," he says, "that's what I'll do."
No point arguing with that voice either.

Mom's back to she-bear. "If Bryan or Cyril
look at you sideways, they'll have me to deal with.
And I still think we should lay charges, Bertram."
"Nix will deal with it," Dad says.
She sloshes more coffee into Dad's mug.
"I'll *never* understand the men in my family."

Carefully, because my face is sore,
I grin at her. "Men, huh?"

"Bryan Sykes—*such a lovely young man,
so charming.* How could I have been so stupid?"
"He's a pro at charm, Mom."
"Thank you, Nixon, but that's no excuse."

She fastens her eyes to mine. "There's something else
I need to say. Roxanne's accident wasn't your fault.
She always broke the rules—clothes, makeup, boys—
        one fight after another. We didn't realize
she slept with Bryan, or that she drank,
but I'm not surprised. Drugs...we didn't make any rules
about drugs in case she ran straight to the nearest dealer."
"She never did drugs," I say quickly.

Dad takes over. "You'd tell on her when you were little
because she'd hidden your Tonka truck
or stolen your Smarties.
'Don't be a tattletale,' that's what I used to say.
                        And I meant it."
"Smarties aren't the same as booze!"
"Your sister was reckless. She looked
for trouble, and Bryan Sykes was trouble."
He gazes into his mug. "They were a perfect match."

"I knew Bryan was trouble
from the get-go, Dad! But I never let on."
"If I'd grounded her from now until kingdom come,
she'd have found a way to see him—
we couldn't watch her twenty-four seven. No one could."

I dig my nails into the place mat.
"I should've gone with her to the party—I knew
Bryan was putting the moves on another girl."
"You think she'd have let you? Her kid brother?
Nix, this is Roxy we're talking about."

Bryan. It's like he blindsided her.

I look up. Mom and Dad are both watching me.
"So you don't think it was my fault?"

Mom shakes her head, tears in her eyes.
"If I hadn't been so over-protective,
maybe she'd have confided in me more...
I only regret I couldn't reach out to you, Nixon.
I just...couldn't. Last night, your face—
                    it was a wake-up call."

Dad pats her hand, looking like
the old man he'll turn into. "When your mom
said I was too hard on Roxy, too strict, she was right.
We all did the best we could, Nix.
And it wasn't enough."

So all three of us are guilty?
Not sure how I feel about that.

Arms full of milk, dill pickles,

and whole wheat bread, I'm barreling
around the end of the aisle
at Godsell's Convenience and run
straight into—*oh crap, it's Blue.*
The bottle of pickles slips

out of my grasp. I grab for it and
so does she, my elbow collides
with softness and by a miracle
I catch the bottle before it crashes

against the metal shelf. *Softness...*
        her eyes like lasers
ready to melt whatever body parts
get in her way—including my elbow and
red face, one cheek looking like I lost a fight
with a cheese grater. She gasps, "What happened?"

"Rocks. On the beach."
"Oh sure." She steps back. "You never used to be violent—
                    it's why I respected you."
"Only time in my life I ever went looking for a fight
was in the school corridor."
"Everyone knew why Roxy's coffin was closed. Not even Bryan
would do that to your face
on purpose. It must have been a fight."

No way am I telling her about Cyril.
I contemplate dropping the pickles
on the floor, then remember the mess

beef stew made. "The roosting boxes—
they'll be finished next week."
"Thank you," she says stiffly.

I don't want her pissed at me. Again.
I say, "What's your real name?"
"Blue not good enough for you?"
"I just wondered, okay?"
"Catriona Elizabeth."

She walks around me in a wide circle
and disappears down the next aisle.

At the counter Harvey Godsell
says gloomily, "You squashed the bread.
I'm charging you full price."

He has a beard. I used to think he was God
selling groceries. "No problem,"
I say, as if squashed bread was at the top
of Mom's list.
              Violent, eh?
I better buy me a black leather jacket, shades, and
           walk with a swagger.

I hear Mom

climbing the stairs, her step
so different from Dad's. Or Roxy's.

"Can I come in?" she asks.
Twig wags her tail. Mom sits on the bed,
catches sight of Fearce
on my bureau. A sigh wrenches itself
all the way from her toes. "Roxanne loved
that bear," she says. "Its silly grin."

She fidgets with her skirt. "Your father and I
think I should tell you about my father...Neil Ardrich."

"You don't have to."

"He was your grandfather, Nixon,
you should know about him...I was only seven
when he died, so some of this I pieced together
afterward." She starts pleating the skirt.
"He was a restless man, always craving
what was over the horizon.
He'd take a job, get bored in six months,
and move on—I never had a best friend
because we never stayed anywhere long enough.
          He was hauling lobster traps
in Sharkey Bay when he won five hundred dollars
in a lottery. Instead of paying off some of the bills,
     he and my mother
went to Corner Brook for the weekend...
they never came home."

You could drown in the emotions swirling
around Mom. But I gotta say it.
"I saw a photo of you with the Joseys.
A table in it like the one I made for your birthday."

"They were so cold-hearted, so mean of spirit.
The minute I saw your table, it was as if I was back there,
being bullied school because I was a foster kid
who grew up too pretty for her own good."
She shivers. "The boys were always after me—Wes Hurly,
his two brothers, his cousins.

One night when I was seventeen,
the Joseys sent me to the Cash and Carry
for a loaf of bread even though I begged them
not to. Wes cornered me
outside the store...I stuck my nail file
in his hand and ran away as fast as I could.
All the way to the highway and even then
I couldn't stop running."

Her fingers twist in her lap. "I had blisters
and I'd slowed to a walk by the time a truck
pulled over.

Your father at the wheel.
I was young, but I knew *trustworthy*
when I saw it.... I lived with Gerd and Mort
until I was old enough to marry."

Hitchhiking. The wrong driver.
Mom could've ended up in a ditch.

Something else.
I could've had the likes of Wes Hurly for a father.

"Thanks for telling me," I say.

Her face crumples. "No one protected me
                        when I was little.
So I did my best to protect my daughter.
And it didn't work."

I feel so damn helpless.
"You were a good mom," I say. "Still are."

"Nixon, you might look like my father.
But you behave like *your* father."

"Oh." I scratch my scalp and I'm smiling. Cowlick,
as usual, doing its thing.

* * *

Next morning, the Shaker table is standing in the front hall.
No tablecloth. No vase.
Just the glow of cherry wood in the light.

I should feel better.

Mom and Dad—they're tight again. Smooching
every time you turn your back
and sometimes when you don't. Dad and me
in the workshop—Humbolt & Humbolt.

I'm running every second day
with Chase and Twig. They think it's fun.
I don't mind as much
as I let on.

My face has scabbed over but I still look like a mobster
in a B-grade movie.
I told Chase the whole story. He said, "You figure
underneath it all Bryan feels guilty?"
"No."

Walking or running,
I carry a dull ache
everywhere...I don't care what Dad says,
if I'd snitched on Roxy the night of the Penguins game
he'd have grounded her
but good.
And no, I haven't talked to Bryan or Cyril.

There's a whack of info

about Guiseppe Penone
on the Internet. I find another photo
of him, head and shoulders
stuck in the guts of the fallen tree, feet
braced in a pile of chips, big chunks
of wood littering the floor.
     The sapling—
if you look close, you can see
that each branch of
the sapling travels outward
to the knot
where the real branch
          broke off.
Using chisels
and a saw
on the heartwood
of a tree,
he's shaping
what's been lost,
what could be forgotten—

will there ever be
an end
to the gap that's Roxy
will sister
ever be an ordinary word

Me and my dog

teeter over the cobblestones
until the rock changes
to slate.
      No sign of Bryan or Cyril.
I pick up a flat piece, fitting it
to the curve of fingers and thumb.

             My sister on the beach
               skipping rocks.
            leap   leap leap leap leap
           until that final blip, the rock
            zigzagging to the bottom.
   Our t-shirts filled like sails with cold salt wind.
            Our sneakers soggy.

I flick the rock. Count the times it bounces
off the water...eight, nine, ten...
I can't cry here. Not in full view
of the twenty-three families
of Bullbirds Cove.

Light smears the waves, drowns
in foam. Stranded by the tide, jellyfish
bake slowly in the sun. Oh man,
I gotta stop this.
            Thicker scabs, that what I need.

Twig gives her *happy-to-see-you* bark.

I blink fast. Blue is scrambling over the slate. Of course
it's Blue. Who would I want to see less
        than Catriona Elizabeth McCallum?

We look at each other. Her soft lips
aren't saying one word.
            I say, "You've cut your hair again."
"There are three Harlequin ducks
in the surf. They're rare
along this shore."
            Looks like her urge to share
her find is battling with her urge to run
in the opposite direction from Nixon Whelan Humbolt.
Gravel in my voice like Dad's, I say,
"I can't, Blue. I just can't."

Can't what?
Can't keep Roxy in.
Can't let Roxy out.

"It'll get better, Nix," Blue says. "It has to."
"That's *your* theory. But what the hell do you know?"

She pushes Twig's head away
and angles across the cobblestones.

It's like—*oh shit*—it's like I'm still fighting
with Roxy.

I can't stop going into Roxy's room.

One Sunday morning, even though I know
I shouldn't, I open her top drawer.
The box I made for her birthday
is lying on a jumble
of underwear. I lift the lid.

A cigarette butt.
A Tim Hortons' cup, neatly flattened.
A pair of copper earrings
attached to a small white card. *x Bryan*

Under the earrings...three photos.
My grade nine school picture.
My grade eight school picture.
My grade seven school picture.

Stunned, I stare at them.
I can't ever remember her
saying, *Love you, bro.*

She just did.

I've got the house to myself.

Dad and Mom have gone to Corner Brook
with Uncle Mort and Aunt Gerd.
I put Roxy's box on the kitchen table

and hoof it over to Aunt Gerd's,
where I take the key from under the flowerpot
and unlock the door.
In the hutch in the dining room, I root around
until I find what I need.

Back home, I tie Twig to her kennel and lock the back door.
Then I line up
the bottle of Smirnoff Triple Distilled,
four cans of Coke,
and a glass
on the kitchen table.

Pour myself a stiff one, gulp it down.
Pour another, reading the label on the pop can
          between swallows.
Lotta calories.   Should be using Diet Coke.

          I finish the third one   lift my head.   The kitchen
                    turns
                              in a slow circle.   I grip the edge
                                        of the table
          remember how Roxy
                              slopped
          vodka on her t-shirt   and now

I understand why.

When I try to pour   the fourth one
    vodka

       soaks into the place mat

   I can't figure out
where   my   mouth   is

    my head
       clonks on the table

           I'm the one   turning circles

  I stumble

    to   Mom and Dad's   bathroom
                          bang up
     the lid
       throw up

I'm on my knees

      porcelain cool under my good cheek

hangovers are way beyond gross   I shoulda remembered
                        her saying that

      I'll pay for this

  I try to stand up

    lean
       over the basin and retch

                              slimy
                        yellow globs

                              that
                        started out as

                        scrambled
                        eggs

            flush

         turn on the cold tap and jam my head under it
         don't say there's no justice, Rox

later   I don't know how much later

                        I make it back to the kitchen

            Roxy's box still sitting on the table

do people always have brilliant ideas
                        when they're drunk?

            I dump the contents of the box
                        waver my way
                  to the workshop

when she sees me
Twig barks

like she doesn't know who I am

         my brain twangs

As I put the box

       on the bench

    the brilliant idea shudders and shifts.

Bryan Sykes didn't pour booze down Roxy's throat.
Roxy poured booze down Roxy's throat.
She coulda slugged him instead.
She coulda slugged Kristen and her blond streaks.

She coulda walked out stone cold sober.

       Nope. Not our Roxy. She got hammered.

     I pick up the nearest hammer.
         Nice balance.
One thing you gotta say about Dad, he buys decent tools.

I bring it down hard on the lid of the box.
    Hit the edge, not the middle.
The bevel splits.
Next stroke strikes the box dead center.
Lid breaks in two.
Four more blows,
the sides smashed flat.
Turn the box upside down
pound the base
crack of wood
shards of maple and walnut—
dovetails shattered—

I stagger

to the other side of the bench.

Six picture frames
so a guy can admire photos of his sister's graduation,
                                                    her wedding,
                    his nieces and nephews,
            her smiling and happy and proud and

                                        alive, goddammit—
why did you *do* this to me, Roxy?
                        Drink yourself blind,
walk into the rain, into the middle of
                        the road, into the truck,
            leaving me
            to carry
            the last words I ever spoke to you
            for the rest of my life.

I lift the first picture frame—
we're all framed in wood, our stupid little lives—
smash it against the bench.
            It only hinges
so I smash it harder.
        It snaps in two. Take the hammer
                        to the second frame,
            the third,
        splintered wood, no tidy rectangles for her face,
                                        her smiling face,

Rox
     you shouldn't have
          you shouldn't
               you...

My chin falls to my chest.

The door. Someone's knocking on the door.

My head jerks up.
The room spins.
*Roxy's gonna...*Blue steps in.

I'm swaying on my feet and God knows what I look like.

Blue's face...she walks around the band-saw
and puts her arms around me.

> I hide my face in her hair.
> Her shampoo smells of apples.

My tongue feels thick. "Took me all this time
to get mad at her—guzzled half a bottle of vodka."

Blue's arms tighten.

Weird how it's not sexy. It's—
comforting.

I dunno how long we stand there
before I lift my head and see
the wreckage on the bench.

Up to now, my eyes were dry.
"Shit, Blue, I smashed her box...took me hours to make.
She liked it...kept stuff in it."

Blue links her fingers with mine.

"I'm losing it," I say.
"No, you're not. We'd better clean up the mess."

I blow my nose. "Lotsa time tomorrow..."

"Why don't you keep the bigger fragments?" she says. "Maybe
you could make something out of them."

"Inlay—that's all they're good for."

She gathers the decent-sized pieces in a little pile.
Fiend of a headache clamped around my forehead.
"Why d'you always wear such ugly clothes?"

She laughs, a laugh so real
I wish I could frame it. "Camouflage, on the barrens.
If you ever ask me for a date,
I promise I won't wear my birding shorts."

I gape at her. My brain's throbbing
like my heart's migrated to my head.
She sweeps the rest of the wood
into the garbage. "I'll walk you back to the house."

On the way, she lets Twig off the rope.

Bottle of vodka on the table. My stomach heaves.

Blue pours the rest of it down the sink, rinses the empty bottle
and drops it in her pack, puts the cans in the recycle
and the place mat in the laundry hamper.
"There," she says. "Want me to help you upstairs?"

With Suzie and her crew, that'd be a come-on. But Blue
meant what she said and no more. In a weird way,
that's comforting too.

"I'll be okay. Why'd you come to the workshop?"
"Roosting boxes," she says. "I'll get them another time."
"Good thing I didn't smash those."

The house is quiet
except for Twig drinking from her bowl. A guy and a girl alone
in a house—why is that different from the same guy and girl
alone on the barrens?

"Thanks, Blue. I—well, thanks."

I've got this urge to slide my fingers over her cheekbone.
Hand heavy as mahogany.
She smiles at me and she's gone.

I climb the stairs one
by one,
clutching the railing,
and fall flat on my face on the bed.

Next Morning. Hangover City.

9:06 a.m. Already a hot day.
Dad's taken it into his head
I should prep some oak boards.
I haul them from the rack
to the bench beside the table saw,
sweating straight Smirnoff.
Quadruple Distilled.

When Dad lifts the lid of the garbage
to throw in the rough ends,
he sees the splintered wood. He says, real quiet,
"You okay, Nix?"
"Yeah," I say, "I'm okay."

And apart from a wicked headache and a gut
pitching like a longliner in a gale-force wind,
    I am okay.
Something settled yesterday.
Dunno if I'll ever quit missing Roxy,
but...it feels different.

* * *

I'm gonna find out how you do inlay.
Take the fragments of her box
and fit them into a three-part frame
for the photos she'd saved of her brother.

A February morning

and we're waiting for the school bus, Roxy
and me. We've had a fight—can't remember
what about—so we're standing on opposite sides
of the driveway.

Dropping from the sky, a blizzard
of small birds
settles on the drifts in the ditch.

They're white, flecked with rust and black,
their weight bending
the stems of weeds and grasses.

They peck seeds, peck grit
from the middle of the road,
chattering to themselves.

Roxy and me, we smile at each other.

Like one, the birds lift
into the cold air,
little missiles
with wings.

The Hidden Life Within—

that's the name of Penone's exhibition in Toronto.
I gotta go there, gotta see for myself
what he found
inside that tree uprooted
in a storm, hauled away in a truck, that
dead tree.
           I could use the Driver's Ed
money and my savings
from last summer. Can you fly
Deer Lake to Toronto? Where
would I stay?
           Blue's mom
has quilts in a gallery in Toronto,
she'd know.

I've never been off the Rock.

Dad'll help me—Dad, who went
from fish shacks and garbage boxes
to Windsor chairs
    that are beautiful
and strong enough
to hold you.
        Do all of us
have hidden lives? Roxanne did.
Roxy? She kept turning everything upside down,
    searching.

Seems to me Blue's
found hers.
    What'll happen
if I go looking for mine?

I head to the mall entrance,

                        pavement
simmering in the heat. Bryan Sykes
is walking toward me. He doesn't tower over me
like he used to. I'd like to take a chisel
to his face.
                    He's wearing a Ralph Lauren shirt,
a polo player stitched on the pocket.
"Wait up, Bryan," I say.
He stops. His eyes dart around to see who's nearby.

I say, "I finally figured something out.
Roxy getting drunk at Suzie's party—
you didn't pour pink coolers down her throat.
She did."
He says, "You think I give a shit?"
In a surge of adrenaline—I can feel the truth of it—
I say, "You and Cyril—don't ever mess with me again."

His eyes drop.
I walk past him, work on unclenching
my fists.

Five minutes later I'm in Mark's Work Wearhouse
                    looking at t-shirts but not really seeing them.
I'm gonna kill the sonofabitch...
I started that fight
in a school corridor
where I'd be stopped long before
I could kill anyone.

I won't take a chisel to Bryan's face.

So what does that make me,
coward or hero?
Or somewhere in between,
which is where most of us hang out
most of the time.

It's early,

the sky to the east filleted
     like a salmon.
Me and Twig set out for the gully
where Blue showed me the yellow bird.

We've got the place to ourselves.
What did I expect? That she'd turn up
because I want her to?

We move away from the trees.
While Twig visits her favorite bog hole,
     I scan the barrens.
Near the falls at Seven Days Work, I see
movement. A moose?
Wish I had binocs.

I take the trail to the falls, tripping
over roots because I'm watching that dark spot
come closer.

Two legs, not four.
Blue.
Am I really gonna ask her for a date?

She keeps walking.
So do I.

Twig cocks her ears, then rushes ahead
with little *wuffs* of excitement.

Helluva lot easier being a dog than a guy.

Blue bends

to rub Twig's head.
Brown shorts, gray t-shirt.
I remember how my elbow hit
        softness.

I put one foot in front of the other.
Pitcher plants, their burgundy flowers
sharp-edged as inlay.

The smile Blue gave Twig
wavers
because I'm not smiling.

Her reef-blue eyes.

I walk right up to her,
lean down
and kiss her on the lips.
Her eyes wide now,
                startled,
her cheeks flushed. My face—
for once—doesn't feel red.
But my heart's pumping like
I just climbed Seven Days Work.

I reach for her hand, my hand
sliding down her arm. Her skin
smoother than planed maple, and warm.

My fingers dovetail with hers.

What did you think when you saw
the sapling carved from heartwood?
What do you want to be when you leave school?
Is the yellow warbler still around? And those ducks
bending the rules off Bullbirds Cove, have they flown away?

I say, my voice hoarse, "Roxy and me,
we had a major fight
before she walked out the door
for the last time."

"Oh, Nix," she says.

I lift our joined hands, stare
at the white scars on my knuckles.
"I loved my sister.
Still do. Alive or dead
doesn't change that.
She loved me, too—
I know she did."

When I reach for Blue's other hand,
her fingers curl around mine.
"Do you think Roxy'd forgive me
those ugly words I threw in her face? Words
        I can't take back."
"Of course she would!"
"Letting myself off the hook—
            that's the hard part."
"We all make mistakes."
"You and Chase, do you fight?"
"Do birds fly?"
"I couldn't tell Mom. Or Dad. Had to be you."
"That's because we're friends."

If it's only about friendship, why couldn't I tell Chase?

Tears are hanging on Blue's lashes.
                  I stroke her cheekbone
as though I've been touching girls
all my life, but this is Blue and it feels
easy and right and
churns me up something fierce. "Why'd you hang in
after Roxy died? I kept dumping my crap on you—
it was like you were
safe, what kind of excuse is that?"

She bites her lip. "The morning
you made the dovetails, the way you and the wood
were connected...and Nix, your sister had died."
"So you felt sorry for me."
"It's not that simple! I can't imagine how I'd feel
        if anything happened to Chase."

I hesitate. Try to sound jokey, but it doesn't come off.
"Am I forgiven?"
"Yes," she says.

We walk hand in hand
to a granite ridge. Twig finds another bog hole,
gulps some water, wades in. I want me and Blue
to be more than friends.
           Likely she already knows
what I want—no flies on Blue—
but I gotta find the nerve to spit it out.
                  "Will you
go out with me? To the movies? Next weekend?"

"I'd love to." She's smiling. "I'll wear
my new brown t-shirt and black shorts."

Yes. She said *yes.*
        "Brown t-shirt with brown shorts," I say,
        "or black t-shirt with black shorts."
She turns serious, so serious
I get nervous. "Would you be okay
if we went out with Chase and Loren?"
Relief washes through me. Is that all? "Sure. It'd be fun.
Not the first time, though."
                        Later,
I'll tell her about Loren. Later I'll thank her
for Guiseppe Penone. By the looks of it, *later*
has a real good chance of happening.
I smile at her, a no-holds-barred smile.

She touches my cheek, where the scabs
are almost gone. "*Were* you fighting with Bryan?"

I force the words out. "Him and Cyril.
        They got hold of me.
        Down at the beach."
She winces. "And I accused you of being violent."
"It's okay."

I put my arms around her, pull her close, kiss her again.
She tastes of sky and spearmint toothpaste.
I'm getting the hang of this
        and it goes clear to my toes
and to all points in between and I don't step away
and yeah, this time my face feels red.

For a while we just stand there, talking about
this and that. The two of us.

Then I say, "Ploughing Bryan, mouthing off at you,
smashing Roxy's box—what do you *do* with anger?

Roxy, she—does falling in love mean you put on blinders?
And if someone threatens to pull them off, is denial
    the only way to go?"
She blinks. "When you talk, Nix, you talk.
Give me a week—or two— to come up with some answers."

"I'll give you a whole year of weeks. If you want."

Our third kiss says what I don't have words for.

Happiness is shining in her face.
Me, Nix Humbolt, I did that.

We untangle ourselves.

Blue says, kind of breathless, like she's not quite ready to know
    how we're discovering more than we expected,
"A few months ago, I saw Roxy put the run on Kendel
when he was bullying Stevie Poole. She was a firecracker—
half Kendel's size and he didn't have a hope."

"I didn't realize she'd even noticed Stevie...you ever wonder
about other people, how it's like we skip rocks over the surface?"

We sit down on the granite ridge.
I put my arm around her and breathe deep.
I begin with Vampire Red,
although it could have been Iron Maiden or copper earrings
or a locked door—there's no real beginning
and no ending, leastways that's how I see it.

Twig shakes herself, lies down in the shade of the rock,
and starts snoring. Roxy is nowhere and
everywhere. Light shivers on the water,
and Blue leans into me.

My warm thanks to:

Jonathan Otter, furniture maker in Earltown, Nova Scotia, who welcomed me to his studio, showed me how to make dovetails, and was kind enough to read the portions of the manuscript that related to woodworking.

Gail Winskill of Pajama Press, for her continued belief in, and support of, my writing.

Ann Featherstone, editor of all my books, who guided me through the pitfalls of characterization, pacing, and innumerable linebreaks with her usual intelligence, honesty, and grace.

Rebecca Buchanan, the Pajama Press designer, for her painstaking attention to typesetting, and her artistic eye for the cover design.

The poetry group—Rose Adams, John Wall Barger, Brian Bartlett, Deirdre Dwyer, Tonja Gunvaldsen Klaassen, Gen Lehr, and Margo Wheaton—for their insightful comments and suggestions.

Dodie, Colin, and Stuart MacLean, who patiently answered questions that ranged from police procedure to Modern Warfare (Stuart always won).

Barbara Markovits, Mary Jo Anderson, Sue MacLeod, and Tonja Gunvaldsen Klaassen, who read and gave me feedback on earlier versions of the manuscript.

The Abbey Girls, to whom I read the initial pages of *Nix Minus One* for the very first time.

Jill MacLean began writing for children later in life and she has quickly made her mark. Among her many awards and honours are an Ontario Library Association Forest of Reading nomination for every one of her titles and an Ann Connor Brimer Award for Children's Literature for both *The Nine Lives of Travis Keating* and *The Present Tense of Prinny Murphy*; the former was also selected for the 2012 IBBY Honour List, and the latter was shortlisted for the Ruth and Sylvia Schwartz Children's Book Award. Jill lives in Bedford, Nova Scotia, and divides her time among writing novels, visiting schools, canoeing, hiking, and pursuing her love of music, reading, and travel.